"So we're both patriots,"

Chase muttered.

To his surprise, Andi laughed. "I guess we are, Remington. See, we have a lot more in common than you thought."

She laughed again as she turned around and kept walking. It was only the relief at getting past the village, he told himself. That was why the sound of her laughter made him feel so giddy. That was why Andi had laughed in the first place. There was nothing more to it than that.

But he knew it wasn't true. Everything had shifted when he'd kissed her and she'd kissed him back. Now awareness hummed between them, and he knew it wouldn't go away until they parted.

Dear Reader,

It's time to go wild with Intimate Moments. First, welcome historical star Ruth Langan back to contemporary times as she begins her new family-oriented trilogy. *The Wildes of Wyoming—Chance* is a slam-bang beginning that will leave you eager for the rest of the books in the miniseries. Then look for *Wild Ways*, the latest in Naomi Horton's WILD HEARTS miniseries. The first book, *Wild Blood*, won a Romance Writers of America RITA Award for this talented author, and this book is every bit as terrific.

Stick around for the rest of our fabulous lineup, too. Merline Lovelace continues MEN OF THE BAR H with *Mistaken Identity*, full of suspense mixed with passion in that special recipe only Merline seems to know. Margaret Watson returns with *Family on the Run*, the story of a sham marriage that awakens surprisingly real emotions. Maggie Price's *On Dangerous Ground* is a MEN IN BLUE title, and this book has a twist that will leave you breathless. Finally, welcome new author Nina Bruhns, whose dream of becoming a writer comes true this month with the publication of her first book, *Catch Me If You Can*.

You won't want to miss a single page of excitement as only Intimate Moments can create it. And, of course, be sure to come back next month, when the passion and adventure continue in Silhouette Intimate Moments, where excitement and romance go hand in hand.

Enjoy!

Leslie J. Wainger
Executive Senior Editor

Please address questions and book requests to:
Silhouette Reader Service
U.S.: 3010 Walden Ave., P.O. Box 1325, Buffalo, NY 14269
Canadian: P.O. Box 609, Fort Erie, Ont. L2A 5X3

FAMILY ON
THE RUN
MARGARET WATSON

Published by Silhouette Books

America's Publisher of Contemporary Romance

For Meg. Your kindness, your grace and your sweet
thoughtfulness fill my life with light and joy.
I am so proud that you're my daughter. I love you.

SILHOUETTE BOOKS

ISBN 0-373-07988-5

FAMILY ON THE RUN

Copyright © 2000 by Margaret Watson

Visit us at www.romance.net

Printed in U.S.A.

Books by Margaret Watson

Silhouette Intimate Moments

An Innocent Man #636
An Honorable Man #708
To Save His Child #750
The Dark Side of the Moon #779
*Rodeo Man #873
*For the Children #886
*Cowboy with a Badge #904
*The Fugitive Bride #920
*The Marriage Protection Program #951
Family on the Run #988

*Cameron, Utah

MARGARET WATSON

From the time she learned to read, Margaret could usually be found with her nose in a book. Her lifelong passion for reading led to her interest in writing, and now she's happily writing exactly the kind of stories she likes to read. Margaret is a veterinarian who lives in the Chicago suburbs with her husband and their three daughters. In her spare time she enjoys in-line skating, birdwatching and spending time with her family. Readers can write to Margaret at P.O. Box 2333, Naperville, IL 60567-2333.

IT'S OUR 20th ANNIVERSARY!
We'll be celebrating all year, continuing with these fabulous titles, on sale in February 2000.

Special Edition

 #1303 Man...Mercenary...Monarch
Joan Elliott Pickart

 #1304 Dr. Mom and the Millionaire
Christine Flynn

 #1305 Who's That Baby?
Diana Whitney

#1306 Cattleman's Courtship
Lois Faye Dyer

 #1307 The Marriage Basket
Sharon De Vita

 #1308 Falling for an Older Man
Trisha Alexander

Intimate Moments

 #985 The Wildes of Wyoming—Chance
Ruth Langan

#986 Wild Ways
Naomi Horton

 #987 Mistaken Identity
Merline Lovelace

#988 Family on the Run
Margaret Watson

 #989 On Dangerous Ground
Maggie Price

#990 Catch Me If You Can
Nina Bruhns

Romance

 #1426 Waiting for the Wedding
Carla Cassidy

#1427 Bringing Up Babies
Susan Meier

#1428 The Family Diamond
Moyra Tarling

 #1429 Simon Says...Marry Me!
Myrna Mackenzie

#1430 The Double Heart Ranch
Leanna Wilson

#1431 If the Ring Fits...
Melissa McClone

Desire

 **#1273 A Bride for Jackson Powers**
Dixie Browning

#1274 Sheikh's Temptation
Alexandra Sellers

#1275 The Daddy Salute
Maureen Child

#1276 Husband for Keeps
Kate Little

#1277 The Magnificent M.D.
Carol Grace

#1278 Jesse Hawk: Brave Father
Sheri WhiteFeather

Chapter 1

The village was too damn quiet.

Chase Remington stood in the shadows at the edge of the Central American village of Chipultipe and waited. But he heard nothing.

There were no voices or music drifting out of the village tavern, which should have been full of people at this hour of the night.

There were no people on the streets.

No babies cried and no dogs barked.

It was as if the darkness of night had pressed down on Chipultipe, smothering all signs of life.

Adrenaline surged through Chase as he waited in the darkness. The hot humid air was heavy with expectation. It was a feeling he understood and respected. It had saved his life more than once in his years as an agent.

But he wasn't an agent any longer, he reminded himself. He touched the gun that nestled at the small of his back. He was only a private investigator, hired to do a specific job here in Chipultipe.

He didn't care what was going on in this village, unless it had something to do with the woman and the kid he was supposed to take to the city. And he doubted that a woman and her baby were the source of the tension that permeated the very air of this village.

He moved out of the shadow only long enough to blend into another one. He knew exactly where to find Paloma Juarez. And it was past time to grab her and her kid and get the hell out of this place. He wanted to be back in his bed and sound asleep in his luxury hotel in Monterez before dawn.

Moving soundlessly from alley to alley, he made his way to the small house where Paloma Juarez lived. He paused outside the door, then nodded when he heard the quiet murmur of a woman's voice. It sounded as if she was crooning to a baby. He took one more look around the deserted street, then slipped in through the door.

The woman's voice stopped abruptly. Knowing she must have heard him, Chase hurried toward the other room in the small house to reassure her. But when he stepped into the tiny room, now completely dark, he saw no one.

''Don't move.''

The voice came out of the shadows, harsh and guttural in the Spanish dialect of the region. He whipped his head around toward the source of the voice—and froze when he saw the gun aimed at his heart and held in a hand as steady as a rock.

"You're making a mistake," he said. He heard a sharp gasp. The gun wavered for a moment, then pointed at his heart once again.

"What are you doing here?" She remained hidden in the darkness.

"I'm looking for Paloma Juarez," he said as he stared intently into the shadows. Something about that voice was hauntingly familiar, making his nerves hum and his blood quicken. "Her uncle sent me to bring her and her baby to Monterez."

The silence quivered for a moment. "You're too late," the voice finally said, and there was no mistaking its bitterness. "Paloma is gone."

He *knew* that voice. "Who are you?" he asked. "And where the hell did she go?"

A woman stepped out of the shadows and the gun disappeared. "Paloma didn't go anywhere," she said, speaking now in English.

Chase stared at the woman who stood in front of him. Her black hair was shorter than it was the last time he'd seen her, but he hadn't forgotten her face. His heart slammed into his ribs, and a vise squeezed his chest. Desire, carefully leashed for three years, ripped at him with savage teeth.

"Andrea McGinnis. What the hell are you doing here?"

"I was just about to ask you the same thing, Remington."

"I was hired to come here and get Paloma Juarez and her kid."

"And I've been here all along." Her look was measuring. "Didn't Mac tell you that?"

"Mac had nothing to do with this job."

"Mac Andrews was the only person besides me who knew about Paloma. If someone hired you to get her out, it could only have been Mac."

Anger burned through him, and Chase welcomed it. It helped fight the unwanted desire that threatened to swamp him. It was better to focus on Mac and his scheming.

His former boss had used him, and done it very cleverly. By baiting him with a huge payment and working through a third party, he'd succeeded in getting him back to the country of San Marcos.

He let the anger flow through him. It cleansed him of his unwanted yearning for Andrea—or Andi, as she preferred to be called. He'd never allowed himself to think of her as anyone but McGinnis. It would be foolhardy and dangerous to think of her any more personally than that.

Then he forced himself to put aside both his anger and his memories of Andi. He didn't have time for any emotions right now. All he wanted was to get out of this town. "It doesn't matter who sent me. All I want is Paloma Juarez and her kid."

She turned away abruptly. "And I told you, Paloma isn't going anywhere."

"There must have been a reason for Mac to fix up

this elaborate charade. He must want her out of here pretty badly.''

''He did. But it's too late. Paloma is dead.''

Her words hit him like a fist, but he controlled his reaction. Regrets wouldn't change a thing. ''What about the kid?''

Andi reached under the bed and pulled out a small blanket-wrapped bundle, holding it to her chest. ''Paolo is safe, and he's going to stay that way.''

Andi glared at him, but he saw the faint glitter of tears on her cheeks. ''What happened?'' he asked more gently.

She shook her head. ''I don't have time to explain. Paolo and I have to leave now.'' She set the baby gently on the floor, then grabbed a backpack and shrugged in on.

''I'll take you to Monterez.''

''No, thanks. We can't risk going over the roads.''

''Then how are you going to get there?''

She gave him a cool look. ''I think it's better if you don't know.''

She started to brush past him, but he reached out and grabbed her wrist. That was a mistake. Her skin was as soft as he remembered. And her wrist was delicate, the tiny bones vulnerable in his huge hand. If he didn't know that Andi McGinnis was as tough as a jungle vine, he'd mistake her delicacy for weakness. But he knew there was nothing weak or vulnerable about Andi McGinnis.

She froze when he touched her. When she turned to look at him, he thought he saw a flash of panic in her deep blue eyes. It was quickly hidden. "Let me go."

"You're not going anywhere until you tell me what's going on."

"I told you, Remington, Paolo and I don't have time for explanations. We have to get out of Chipultipe."

"And I said I would take you to Monterez. We'll be there by morning."

She shook her head and pulled her wrist free. But his hand still burned with the memory of her soft smooth skin.

"We can't go by road." She touched her wrist with her other hand, and Chase wondered if her skin tingled, too. "He'll have the roads watched."

"Who is 'he'?"

She gave him an impatient look. "Didn't they even tell you that? El Diablo, of course."

His mouth settled into a grim line. "No one told me anything. But I should have figured El Diablo was involved the minute I recognized you."

Her mouth hardened. "I'd love to stand around and swap El Diablo stories with you, but Paolo and I have other plans. Take it easy, Remington."

She bent to pick up the baby and headed into the other room. He moved quickly to stand between her and the door of the house. "You're not going anywhere, McGinnis."

She started to respond, but suddenly stopped. He heard it, too—the sound of men's voices echoing between the houses. It was a sharp contrast to the strained silence he'd felt in the village when he'd first arrived.

Andi's arms tightened around the baby she held, and her eyes flashed at Chase. "Get out of the way, Remington. That's my cue to leave."

"Who are they?"

"El Diablo's men."

It took just an instant for him to make the decision. "Where to?"

"The jungle. It's our only chance."

The instant understanding and connection bothered him, but he didn't have time to analyze it. He pulled open the door and looked down the street. Still empty. Andi slid out beside him, then tilted her head in the direction of the shouting. "That way."

He wanted to argue with her, but she knew the village better than he did. So he followed her silently. She slipped between two houses set very close together and disappeared into a blackness more complete than the deepest pit of hell.

"In here." Her voice was disembodied, and he reached out to find a boxlike structure in front of him, about half as tall as a house. "You'll have to bend down to get in."

The box was hot and cramped and smelled overpoweringly of animals. "What in the blazes is this?"

"It's Miguel Fuertes's old chicken coop. He sold all his chickens last week and hasn't replaced them. It's a perfect place to hide. They won't think to look here, and they'll be past us in a moment."

The voices and shouting were coming closer, and

Chase reached around to pull out his gun. One of Andi's legs pressed against his, making the chicken coop far too warm. He tried to move away, but there was no room. The baby whimpered once, and she murmured something to him in a low voice. The alluring mysterious scent of Andi McGinnis filled his head, a scent that had disturbed his dreams for the past three years. The smell of the chickens seemed to fade away.

As soon as the voices were past their hiding place, Andi squirmed her way to the door and slipped out. Chase followed, his gun drawn.

When she turned to him, he could see the worry on her face. "We don't have much time. I heard what they said, and they're looking for me. It's not going to take them long to realize that Paolo is gone. They'll know I took him."

"What's the quickest way into the jungle?"

"Straight back a few blocks."

"Then let's go."

It looked like she wanted to refuse, but she finally nodded. He turned and moved beyond the chicken coop, then slid into the shadows next to another house.

The village had been hacked out of the jungle, and the trees crowded the perimeter of the town, as if waiting for their chance to snatch the land back. Chase kept Andi and the baby close to him as they moved away from the sound of the men's voices and toward the cover of the vegetation.

They moved between houses and down alleys,

keeping away from the streets. They blended into the night, melting into the darkness and clinging to the shadows. Most of the people in this farming village would have been asleep already, but he wasn't going to take any chances.

Chase paused frequently, shielding Andi and the baby with his body as he looked around. Every time they heard voices Andi tensed. He felt her muscles tighten, felt her hold the baby more closely. He moved through the darkness as quickly as he could.

When they finally reached the last houses at the edge of town, Chase pushed his way into the mass of dense vegetation, holding back the branches and vines so Andi could follow him. She stumbled over exposed roots. He knew that several small branches whipped back and struck her, but she kept up with him, clutching the bundle that was the baby to her chest.

The air was hot and still, smothering him almost as soon as they stepped into the jungle. Humidity settled over him like a wet blanket, making it hard to breathe. Chase felt himself begin to sweat and realized that in minutes his clothes would be soaked through. But he didn't stop. The sound of those angry voices still echoed in his ears. They had to be farther away from the village before they could take a chance on stopping.

Clearly Andi thought so, too. He heard her breathing heavily behind him, but she didn't say a word. And she didn't slow down. Thank God the kid didn't make a sound.

Finally, when they hadn't heard any noise from the

village for a long time, Chase slowed, then stopped. Andi bumped into him and immediately backed away.

Every muscle in his body tightened at the brief contact, and the touch of Andi's slight body lingered on his. He imagined that he could feel every curve, every soft yielding place on her body imprinted on his much larger frame.

The reaction shocked Chase. Andi McGinnis was the last woman in the world he was interested in. She was the last woman in the world he would ever trust. And he wanted her to be the last woman in the world he would ever notice.

But his body seemed to have other ideas.

"Stop here," he said gruffly. "Let's catch our breath and listen for a few minutes."

She sank to the ground and opened the blanket protecting the baby. "Is the kid all right?" he asked after a moment.

She glanced up at him and nodded. "He looks fine. He fell asleep."

"Thank God."

She nodded and whispered, "I was so afraid he was going to start crying."

"It's okay if he cries now. No one can hear him."

She gazed down at the sleeping baby. "I think he's going to sleep for a while."

"You're not sure?"

"I don't know. I've never kept him all night. I don't even know if he sleeps through the night." She touched the baby's cheek lightly, then shifted him in her arms.

Chase shifted back so that he was leaning against a tree. He ignored the stutter his heart made as he watched her caress the baby. "You don't know much about him."

He saw her hold on the child tighten. "I know enough."

"You were planning on taking a kid you know nothing about and running into the jungle with him?"

"I know all I need to know. I've been taking care of Paolo during the day for the past two months."

"That's not the same as taking care of him twenty-four hours a day."

Even in the dim mottled light he saw the stubborn set of her mouth. "It can't be that tough. I'll figure it out."

"Why were you getting ready to take off with him?"

She sighed and glanced down at the baby, and he saw her lower lip quiver. When she looked up at him, he saw the defiance in her eyes. "Because now I'm all he has. And I wasn't going to stay in Chipultipe and watch him get killed."

"Who would kill a little baby?"

Her mouth thinned. "El Diablo. You should know enough about him to know that he wouldn't hesitate to kill an innocent child."

Chase sank to the ground across from her. Weak moonlight filtered through the trees, and there was just enough illumination for him to see her high cheekbones and wide-spaced eyes, but not their expression. He remembered the bright blue color that used to shine like a flame, then he abruptly looked away. He didn't want to notice anything about Andi, including how she looked in the moonlight.

"Tell me what happened to Paloma."

"Don't you think we need to get farther away from Chipultipe?"

"We're safe enough here for the time being. Now I need to know what's going on."

Her eyes flashed at him and now he could read her perfectly. She wanted to tell him that he wasn't in charge, that he had no right to ask questions. But she took a deep breath, instead.

"I owe you that much, I guess."

Andi looked down at Paolo, asleep in her arms, and touched his cheek again. A look of fierce love and protectiveness filled her face, and in spite of himself, Chase's heart moved in his chest. *Get over it,* he told himself.

"I've been here in Chipultipe for the past two months," Andi began. "My cover was as a teacher, sent by the Peace Corps. I was really here to collect information from Paolo's mother, Paloma. She worked as a maid in El Diablo's hideaway."

Chase frowned at her. "How the hell did you hook up with her?"

"She was a very courageous woman," Andi said quietly. "Her husband worked for El Diablo, too. When he was killed by government soldiers during a botched drug delivery several months ago, she finally saw how heartless and cruel El Diablo was. He didn't care about her husband's death—it was just a cost of

doing business for him. She knew she had to stop El
Diablo before any more women lost their husbands.
She managed to call the police on a trip to Monterez,
and they put her in touch with our agency. A couple
of months later I was sent to Chipultipe to act as her
contact.''

"So she was working in El Diablo's house?''

Andi nodded. ''Apparently after her husband died,
El Diablo figured she'd be loyal to him because she
didn't have any choice. She was able to get us some
very valuable information. She didn't think he knew
what she was doing.'' Andi's mouth thinned. ''She
said that El Diablo assumed she would be too grateful
for the work to ever turn on him. Maybe she was
wrong. Or maybe he was just suspicious because a
stranger was taking care of Paolo for her, and he
didn't want to take any chances. She was shot as she
walked home this evening and left for dead along the
side of the road.''

Chase leaned forward and touched her hand, in
spite of his warning to himself. ''I'm sorry. That must
have been hard.''

"Of course it was hard.'' Her voice was harsh and
he saw the guilt in her eyes. She swallowed before
she spoke again. Chase looked away, remembering
the pain of losing someone he'd worked with, remembering too clearly the guilt he'd felt. And remembering Andi McGinnis's part in that death.

"Somehow Paloma managed to make it to my
house. I knew she'd lost too much blood and wasn't
going to live, but I did everything I could to make

her comfortable. She died a few minutes before you showed up."

"Why did that mean you had to leave?"

She gave him an impatient look. "Her body is in my house. If El Diablo was suspicious of her already, he's going to think that I was her contact. I was a stranger in the village, and an American, too."

"Then why not just get out yourself? Why take the kid?"

"Because he has no one else now." Her voice was fierce, and she looked down at the sleeping baby. "Paolo has no family left. Someone has to care what happens to him."

"Doesn't he have relatives in the village?"

She shook her head. "No, he doesn't. That's why I was taking care of him. Paloma had no one else to ask. And even if he did have family there, I wouldn't have left him. Paloma begged me to take care of him, and I promised her that I would. If I'd left him, El Diablo would very likely have killed him, too, as a lesson to anyone else who considered betraying him."

She hesitated, then said in a low voice, "Paloma gave me some information before she died—vital information. I have to get it to Monterez, and I only have five days. So you see, I had no choice. I had to leave."

Her fingers tangled in the baby's hair, and Chase told himself to look away. He didn't want to see this side of Andi McGinnis. A strange tenderness moved in his chest as he watched her with the baby, a yearning for something he couldn't quite name. He stood up abruptly, turning away from the picture she presented. A family was the last thing he wanted.

"Why didn't you just radio the information to the city?" His voice was harsher than he'd intended.

"I keep my radio hidden in the jungle. We didn't have time to stop and get it just now. And I don't think it would be safe to go back."

"You can use my cell phone," he offered.

Andi shook her head. "That's too risky. It's too easy to eavesdrop on cell phones. I don't want to tip him off that we know about the meeting. I want him there so we can catch him."

Chase scowled, feeling the jaws of the trap closing around him. "So what's your plan?"

"My plan is to get to Monterez. I appreciate the offer of a ride, but you can see that El Diablo's men will be watching the roads. They'll stop everyone and search all the cars. I can't go that way, but you should be perfectly safe if you wait until it's light."

He gave her a measuring look. "So you and the kid are just going to take off through the jungle, by yourselves, hoping to reach the city."

"That about sums it up."

"I don't think so, McGinnis." He shook his head, forced in spite of himself to admire her courage. "I'm afraid you and the kid are stuck with me until we get to Monterez."

"And why would that be?"

He gave her a thin smile. She would never accept the truth, that he didn't want to leave her alone in the jungle. She was too fiercely independent for that. So he said, "I've got a nice chunk of money riding on this job. And Paolo is my paycheck."

Andi narrowed her eyes. "What's going on, Remington? Why are you so interested in Paolo? And don't tell me it's for the money. You don't give a damn about money. I know you better than that."

"You don't know a thing about me, McGinnis." His gaze held hers for a moment, then she looked away. "I was hired to do a job and I'm going to do it. With your cooperation or without it."

"Forget it," she said, and he heard the edge of desperation in her voice. "Paolo and I will be just fine."

He shook his head slowly. "I don't think so, McGinnis. My money says that there's no way you're making it to Monterez by yourself. I'm afraid you're stuck with me."

"Why? We don't need your help. I don't want your help." He heard the beginnings of panic in her voice, and he wanted to snatch back his promise. Andi McGinnis had invaded his memory and haunted his dreams for the past three years. No matter how hard he tried, he hadn't been able to banish her from his mind. Now, watching the uneasiness in her eyes, he wondered if she had thought about him, too. He damn well hoped not.

But in the end it didn't matter. He wasn't about to walk away from her and the baby in this cruel and unforgiving jungle.

"Let's just say I'm feeling like a Good Samaritan

tonight. And you're the lucky recipient of my charity.''

''You've never done anything out of the goodness of your heart in your life,'' she snapped.

He gave her a mocking smile. ''Maybe civilian life has mellowed me.''

''And maybe pigs can fly. Go back to Monterez, Remington.''

''Can't do it, McGinnis. Call it my chivalrous side, but it goes against the grain to leave a woman and a child on their own in the jungle. Even if the woman is you.''

''So you're going to stay with me until we reach Monterez?''

''That's the plan.''

He saw the anger in her eyes, and he also saw the realization that she had no choice. It made for an intriguing mix of temper and frustration. He wondered if he'd see the same mix if he kissed her.

The thought appalled him. He wouldn't ever kiss Andi McGinnis again, he vowed. Especially after their last kiss. He'd learned just how deadly a kiss could be.

Apparently unaware of his thoughts, she stood up. ''We might as well get going, then.''

Chase raised his eyebrows as he unfolded himself from the ground. ''I figured you'd see it my way.''

''I didn't realize I had a choice,'' she said. His heart kicked against his chest when he saw her temper flare again.

''A lady always has a choice,'' he said, his voice

mocking. "Sometimes the choices are less appealing than others."

"Given the choice of you or death, then, I guess I have to choose you." Her eyes flashed at him. "But I had to think about it first."

"It's going to be an interesting trip to Monterez," he said. "Let's get started."

Chapter 2

Andi watched Chase pace the small clearing as she put Paolo into his sling carrier. Then she slung the large backpack over her shoulders and stood up. "We're ready."

Chase stopped pacing and looked down at her. He'd always used his size to intimidate people, but Andi wasn't about to let him intimidate her. She straightened her spine and stared back.

His mouth twitched once, then he moved a step backward. "How did you plan to get to Monterez?" he asked. "You weren't thinking of walking through the jungle, were you?"

"Of course not." She gave him a scornful look and adjusted Paolo in the sling. "There's a river not too far from here. I thought we'd get a canoe and float some of the way. Once we're out of this part of the country, it'll probably be safe to take the roads.''

''Where did you plan on getting a canoe?'' he asked.

She hesitated for only a moment. Chase was right. She and Paolo didn't have a chance on their own. So she sighed and said, ''There's another village about two miles from Chipultipe. It's right on the river. I thought I'd go there, then start walking downriver. I'd planned on taking a canoe from the next village.''

She saw a glimmer of appreciation in his eyes. ''That's smart. El Diablo might tell his men to check the first village, but they'd be less likely to look farther down the river.''

She shrugged off his compliment. ''It sounded like a good idea to me.''

''I probably would have done the same thing.''

His voice sounded grudging. She gave him a sharp look and said, ''High praise indeed. I'll try not to let it go to my head.''

She saw him fight the half smile that curled his mouth. ''You're quick, I have to give you that.'' He glanced down at Paolo, asleep in the sling, and quickly looked away. ''Why don't you stay here and wait with the kid for a while? I'll take a look around. If I remember the map, that river shouldn't be too far away. There's no sense in both of us fighting the jungle.''

After all the stress of the past few hours, her body screamed for rest, for sleep. But she couldn't afford that kind of weakness. Not until they were a lot farther away from Chipultipe. "How will you find us again in the darkness?"

"Worried I won't come back? I thought you wanted to get rid of me."

"It's my fondest wish," she muttered.

And it was. She didn't want to spend any time at all with Chase Remington. The memories from the last time, three years ago, were still too raw and painful. The harsh words he'd spoken were etched into her mind.

And so was Chase himself. His eyes had held nothing but hatred as he'd stared at her. Contempt and derision had filled his face as his gaze swept insultingly up and down her body.

And she remembered her reaction. Even now, her face grew hot with embarrassment as she recalled the quickening of her pulse, the faint stirring of desire. He hated her because of what had happened, and she had still wanted him.

She never knew if he'd noticed her response to him that day.

She'd told herself fiercely that she didn't care.

He had disappeared from her life, but she hadn't forgotten him, no matter how hard she'd tried. Now he was back, and she wanted nothing more than for him to disappear again. Chase was a distraction she couldn't allow herself. The information Paloma had died for was the culmination of twelve years of effort. It was too important to risk any distractions, even Chase Remington.

Especially Chase Remington.

"Get out of here if you're going," she muttered.

He was already turning away, but he pivoted around and squatted in front of her. "Stay here, McGinnis," he ordered. "I don't want to come back and find you gone. It would really tick me off."

"And God knows I don't want to tick you off," she said, her voice mocking. She hoped it hid the way he made her quiver inside.

"Look, McGinnis, getting that baby to Monterez safely is going to be hard enough. Do you want to make it harder by not cooperating with me? Because if we're not working together, we're just making El Diablo's job a lot easier. It's your choice. What's it going to be?"

She held his eyes for a moment, then dropped her gaze to the baby. Paolo shivered in his sleep. She touched his dark hair lightly, then looked back up at Chase.

"Don't worry, I'll be here when you get back. You're right. As much as I don't want to work with you, I don't have a choice. Paolo doesn't deserve to die. I'll go with you to Monterez." She gave him a quick humorless smile. "I'd work with the devil himself to save Paolo."

"I'll keep that in mind, McGinnis."

Andi watched Chase disappear into the dense wall of green that was the jungle. Nothing had changed since she'd last seen him. His blond hair was dark with sweat and longer than she remembered. But his green eyes burned with the same intensity, and he still looked at her with contempt.

And nothing had changed inside of her, either. Her heart still shriveled a little every time his eyes dismissed her. And her soul still longed for what she couldn't have, what she shouldn't even have been thinking about.

She had a mission. She glanced down at the now sleeping Paolo. She had information to get to Monterez and a baby to rescue from a killer. She didn't have time for foolish yearnings that had no basis in reality.

A small voice urged her to leave now, to run away from the threat Chase posed. She wouldn't be able to concentrate on her mission as long as Chase was around. He would be a distraction and a complication she didn't need.

But she couldn't leave. She'd promised Chase she would wait for him, and she would. She prided herself on keeping her word. She thought of her parents for a moment. Standing next to their graves twelve years ago, she'd made them a promise. She intended to keep that one, too.

She'd stretched out on the ground and fallen into a light sleep when a sound roused her. Her arm tightened around Paolo and she silently sat up, pulling her gun out from under her shirt. When Chase stepped into the clearing, she put the gun away.

"You're still here." He sounded surprised.

"I told you I would be."

"Yeah, well, I don't trust too many people."

"I guess we have at least one thing in common,

then,'' she said as she began to gather up the supplies she'd left on the ground. "What did you find?"

He looked at her for a moment and she thought he was going to say something, but instead, he looked away. "The river isn't far. I followed it for a while and didn't see anyone. We'll go as far as we can before stopping—I hope we can reach that second village tonight. There's a narrow path that runs along the river, so we won't be fighting the jungle the whole way." He looked down at the baby. "How do you suppose he's going to be?"

She knew what Chase was thinking—was Paolo going to cry and give away their presence? "I'm not sure," she said slowly. "I fed him a bottle I brought while you were gone and changed his diaper. He's normally a very easygoing baby. But he's not with his mother and he's not sleeping in his own bed. I guess we'll find out."

"I guess we will." Chase looked at her pack, then at the baby. "Let me take some of the things from your pack," he said abruptly.

"Trying to make sure I don't run off on you?" She raised one eyebrow, the challenge in her eyes unmistakable.

"Dammit, McGinnis, I'm trying to make things easier for you." He scowled. "Is it that tough to admit you need help?"

"Not if it was true," she retorted. "And don't blame me if I suspect your motives. Don't forget, Remington, I know how you feel about me."

''You don't know a damn thing about it,'' he muttered.

Her heart stuttered in her chest as she stared at him. But he circled around behind her and opened her pack. He was standing too close, and she felt the heat radiating off his body and smelled his musky male scent. Even in the jungle, surrounded by the strong smell of dirt and vegetation, his scent seemed to engulf her. She felt herself start to tremble and she wanted to move away, but he was holding on to her backpack.

''How does that feel?'' he asked gruffly, and he stepped away.

She wanted to tell him she hadn't felt anything like it in three years, but she bit her lip and said, ''Lighter.'' She tried to keep her voice from quivering.

''Then let's get started.'' He avoided her gaze. ''We'll have to push our way through the vegetation until we get to the river, but after that it should be easier going.''

''Fine.''

Chase stepped into the dense undergrowth, and Andi hesitated a moment before following him. This was not good. She and Chase were going to be spending the next few days together, and she had better learn to hide her reaction to him. At the very least it would be totally humiliating if he realized how he still affected her. At the worst it could be downright dangerous if it distracted her from her job.

She forced herself to concentrate on where she was

going. After a few minutes she couldn't think about anything else. Thick vines reached out to trip her, and thin branches whipped her face. Chase tried to hold them back for her, but it didn't help. Instead of protecting her face, she used her hands to shield Paolo from the branches and the insects that seemed to swarm around his tiny head.

By the time Chase stopped, her face burned and stung from the lashes of countless branches, and sweat dripped down her cheeks. Impatiently she swiped one arm over her face as she peered ahead. The river must be close. There was a hint of a breeze and the smell of water in the air, pungent and faintly fishy.

"We're just about there." Chase moved closer and spoke softly into her ear. She shivered involuntarily and hoped he hadn't noticed. "Let's wait here for a moment and just watch," he added.

She nodded again and prayed he would move away, but he stayed close. His heat enveloped her again, and she could feel the tension in his hard muscles, feel his wariness. But he wasn't looking at her. He was scanning the area around them, assessing their situation.

Don't be a fool, she told herself sharply. Chase Remington was the last man on earth who should be stirring her hormones. He hated her. He hadn't forgiven her for deceiving him three years ago, and she was sure he held her partly responsible for his partner's death.

And he was right. It was her fault Richard Butler was dead.

She took a step away from him, away from the temptation he presented, and tried to grab hold of her galloping emotions. Taking a deep steadying breath, she said, "How close are we to the path you found?"

"You're standing on it," he said.

Andi looked around and saw that there was a faint depression in the ground parallel to the river, and the vegetation wasn't quite as thick. It was the best they could hope for, she realized.

"How's the kid doing?" Chase asked. He still wasn't looking at her.

"Sleeping." She touched Paolo's head, noticing that in spite of her efforts, he had several insect bites. "He's always slept pretty soundly."

"Good." Chase stepped back and finally turned to face her. "Let's start— My God! What happened to your face?"

Andi touched her cheek. "What do you mean?"

"You're covered with cuts, and there's blood smeared all over your cheeks."

He reached out and took her chin in his hand, and Andi's heart jumped in her chest. Her skin burned where his fingers touched her, and she wanted to pull away. Instead, she looked down at Paolo, reminding herself what was at stake if she made a stupid mistake.

"It looks like every branch in the damn jungle sliced across your face," he finally said, letting her go. She drew a ragged breath and moved slightly away from him. "Let's clean them up."

Andi shook her head. "They're fine. We don't have time right now. Don't we need to get moving?" She didn't want Chase to touch her again.

"Do you know how quickly those cuts can get infected in this heat and humidity?" he demanded. "Not to mention all the insects the blood will draw. We're not going a step farther until you're cleaned up."

"I can do it myself," she said, slipping the sling off her shoulders and setting the baby carefully on the ground. "I'll run some water through my purifier and use that."

"Give me the purifier." Chase held out his hand for the thick tube. "You stay here with the kid and I'll get the water."

Before she could object, Chase had plucked the water purifier out of her hand and disappeared into the jungle. Andi took a deep breath, then opened her backpack and rummaged around until she found her first-aid kit. Her hands were hardly shaking anymore, she noticed. She'd clean her face up herself and stay out of Chase's reach.

But when he returned with the clean water in his canteen, he didn't bother to ask her if she preferred to tend to the cuts herself. He simply pulled a T-shirt from his pack and began cleaning her face. His hands were surprisingly gentle.

"How did this happen?" he asked again.

Andi shrugged. She knew why the branches had

snapped into her face time after time, but she had no intention of telling Chase. "I guess there are a lot of branches in the jungle," she said, trying not to think about how his hands felt on her skin.

His hands slowed, then stopped, but he didn't let her go. Instead, his fingers lingered on her cheeks and traced down the side of her face. "I think all the blood is gone."

His voice sounded harsh, and when she glanced at his face, she saw that his skin was drawn tightly over his cheekbones. His eyes, hard and sharp as emeralds, were glowing in the faint moonlight. Desire glittered in their depths.

She told herself to move, but the drumbeat of desire began to beat in her blood, answering what she saw in his face. She stared at him, watching his pupils dilate, and felt the throb of need deep inside her, shocking her with its intensity. Every touch of his fingers on her skin sent a flash of fire through her veins, and she found herself leaning toward him.

He moved closer, his eyes fixed on hers. Then the vegetation rustled beside them, and Chase jerked away from her as if he'd been stung.

He stared at her for another moment, and she could see he was breathing heavily. Her own heart pounded in her chest in an insistent rhythm, and it took all her willpower to look away from him and pick up the first-aid kit.

"Thank you for cleaning the scratches," she managed to say, but her voice sounded high-pitched and breathless. "I'll put some cream on them."

"You do that," he said, getting to his feet and turning away from her. "Then we'll start walking again."

It only took a moment to smear some of the white cream on her face, then she stowed the kit in her backpack and picked up the still-sleeping Paolo. Her hands were shaking, she noted, and her legs felt weak and rubbery.

"Drink the rest of this water," Chase said, and he handed her the canteen. "I don't want to stop again until we get a lot farther away."

She drank the water wordlessly, then put the empty canteen into his outstretched hand. She was careful not to touch him.

He turned around and began walking, and she scrambled to keep up with him. Although the path was narrow, it was apparently well used, because there were very few branches that slapped at her as she walked. It was much easier to keep Paolo's head protected and keep the vines from whipping her own face.

Chase walked quickly, and she had to strain to keep up with him. But she didn't say a thing. She knew as well as he did how important it was to get as far away from Chipultipe as possible. Their lives and Paolo's depended on it.

Chase listened to Andi behind him, hurrying to keep up with his much longer strides. He was walking as if the devil himself was on his tail, because that was the way he felt.

What the hell is the matter with you? Chase asked himself.

He'd come too damn close to kissing Andi Mc-Ginnis. He'd been mesmerized by the blue of her eyes, the hint of startled passion he'd seen in their depths. And his hands still burned with the memory of her soft smooth skin. He'd wanted to let his hands trail down her body, to touch every inch of her. He'd wanted to lay her down on the ground and cover her slim body with his.

He'd wanted the one woman in the world he couldn't have.

He blew out a sharp breath and reminded himself again who Andi was. She was the agent his boss had sent to spy on him and his partner. Someone in their organization had been working for El Diablo and his boss had suspected him and his partner. She had deceived both of them, and he'd played right into her hands by falling for her. He'd been too distracted on their last job to focus completely, and his partner had paid the price. Now Richard was dead, and Andi was part of the reason why. And he'd better not forget it again.

He wouldn't allow himself to be distracted this time. This time he would ignore the way his body reacted to Andi McGinnis. He was here to do a job, and he would damn well do it. Andi was just part of that job.

An inner voice whispered that she was far more than that, but he paid no attention. Andi was not to be trusted—which she'd already proved. And he'd better not let his hormones forget it again.

"We should be getting close to the village," Andi

said behind them, her breathless voice a prick to his conscience.

"Is it on this side of the river?"

"No, the other. But I'm pretty sure there are farm plots on this side, so we need to be careful. There won't be any cover to hide us."

Chase slowed down, too aware of Andi right behind him. Her scent seemed to cling to the air around her, urging him closer.

"How close do you think we are?" he said roughly, trying to ignore the throbbing of his body.

"No more than a quarter mile." She spoke in a harsh whisper, even though the sounds of the jungle at night would muffle her voice. "If my calculations are correct, there should be a bend in the path just ahead of us, then suddenly you're in the fields."

Chase slowed down even more, and in a few moments he saw the bend. He stopped and touched her arm, pulling back sharply when his blood fired again at the feel of her skin.

"Let's go into the jungle again, until we know what we'll find in the village."

She nodded in agreement, waiting for him to lead the way off the path. He plunged into the vegetation and heard her right behind him. When he looked back, he realized why her face had gotten so scratched and cut.

Instead of blocking the branches from her face, her hands formed a protective tent over the sleeping baby. She flinched each time a branch whipped her face, but she didn't take her hands off the baby.

His heart moved in his chest and he grabbed her arm. "Walk next to me. I'll keep the branches off your face."

"I'm fine," she said, pulling away from him. "It's more efficient for me to walk behind you."

"Don't be an idiot." His voice was rough with emotion. She was allowing herself to be injured in order to protect Paolo. "I won't bite."

She glanced at him out of the corner of her eye. "That's news to me."

"You just watch out for the kid, and I'll watch out for you," he retorted.

"And who's going to watch out for you?"

"I can take care of myself."

They moved more slowly through the jungle, but he noticed with satisfaction that the branches no longer hit her face. They both apparently heard the sound of rushing water at the same time, because she stopped before he could put out a hand. As if they thought with one mind, both crouched at the same time.

He put aside the whisper of uneasiness at their apparent unspoken communication. Creeping through the undergrowth, Andi right next to him, he stopped when he could see the water through the plants. He signaled to her, but she had seen it, too.

Carefully he edged forward until he could see the river clearly. On the other side stood a small village. Lights gleamed from a few of the windows, but there were no sounds coming from the circle of houses.

Suddenly Andi grabbed his arm. Her fingers

gripped tightly, and she pointed to the far edge of the village.

A man stood there, holding an automatic weapon, scanning the river in front of him. As they watched, three other men joined him, all holding efficient-looking weapons.

"El Diablo's men," Andi said in a low voice.

Chapter 3

Chase stared at the four men and nodded without taking his eyes off them. She was right. The men had the hard faces and soulless eyes of killers. Chase had no doubt they were looking for Andi and Paolo.

"Looks like El Diablo thought the same way you did."

"He didn't get to be as powerful as he is because he's stupid," she said.

Chase didn't answer as he watched the men across the river. They were scanning the jungle carefully, their eyes moving steadily back and forth. "Let's move back farther into the jungle," he said in a low voice. "I don't want to be this close if the kid starts crying."

Andi checked on Paolo. "Yes. He's still sleeping,

but I have no idea how long he'll stay that way." Chase heard the worry in her voice. "It would be a good idea to get away from here."

"Start backing up," he ordered, still watching the men across the river. "I'll wait and see if they notice anything."

She started to object, then began to move backward. Too slowly, he thought, and he wanted to tell her to hurry. If the baby started crying, it was all over.

Finally she was far enough away that he couldn't hear her moving through the dense bush. After one more look at the men, he starting backing in to the jungle, too. He was almost out of sight when he heard Paolo wail. It was almost immediately cut off, but he froze and looked at the four men on the far bank of the river.

One of them had jerked around to stare at his hiding place. As Chase watched, the man slowly brought up his gun, still staring across the river. He said something to the other three men. They looked over toward his hiding place, also.

Chase pulled his gun out of its holster smoothly, then stood still and waited. He didn't hear any more sounds from behind him, and after a while he wondered if the wail had been Paolo, after all.

The men apparently felt the same way, because they finally lowered their weapons and turned to walk away. Chase watched as the first man looked over his shoulder once more before they all disappeared into the village.

He waited a long time before he moved. He saw

the men again, but they appeared to be checking all the houses in the village. No one looked toward his hiding place.

Finally he began to move. Slowly and deliberately he headed away from the river, until he could no longer hear the rushing water. When he reached the path, he waited again for long minutes before he crossed it. Once across the path, he moved more quickly. He wondered if Andi was worried, then told himself it didn't matter.

He almost walked right past her. She sat between the roots of a huge tree, foliage almost completely concealing her. He'd hardly given it a second glance when he heard her whispering, "Chase! Over here."

He spotted a flash of movement at the base of the tree and pushed through the veil of vines that concealed it. Andi sat with her back against the tree, Paolo on her lap. Two empty bottles sat on the ground next to her.

"I'm sorry he cried like that," she said, and he saw worry and fear in her eyes. "Did anyone hear him?"

Chase hesitated. "I'm not sure," he finally said. "One of the guys standing by the river heard something, but I think he decided it was an animal. The four of them watched for a long time, but they eventually left. It looked like they were checking all the houses."

She nodded, and he thought her face looked pale. "He opened his mouth and let out that scream without any warning. I gave him his bottle, and he stopped instantly. I guess he was just hungry.'' She looked down at the baby and smoothed a finger down his cheek. ''This must be frightening for him. He's being cared for by strangers and nothing about his surroundings is familiar.''

''Do you think he knows the difference?'' Chase asked.

''Of course he does.'' Her eyes flashed. ''He's four months old. He's very aware of his surroundings. He knows I'm not his mother.''

''Well, he'd better get used to us pretty damn quickly. If you had been closer to the river, those goons would have known for sure we were around.''

''I'll try to be more observant,'' she said, her voice tight.

He sighed and ran his fingers through his hair. ''Hell, McGinnis, it's not your fault. I'm not blaming you.''

''No one is to blame. But I have to get better at anticipating Paolo. Until I do, all three of us are at risk.''

She shifted the baby so she was holding him more closely, an unconscious act of protection. She looked down at Paolo again and her face softened. His heart contracted. For just a moment Chase let himself see the tenderness and yearn for some of it himself.

Then he stood up. Trying to ignore the feeling, he turned and peered out into the endless darkness in front of them. It was no use wishing for what you couldn't have. He'd learned that early in life.

When he could look back at them without wanting

to scoop them both into his arms, he turned around again. "I have a bad feeling about this," he said abruptly. "I don't want to try to get past the village right now. Let's give those men a chance to get out of the village before we go anywhere." He gestured to the baby. "Will he be all right if we stay here for a while?"

"I'm not sure," she said slowly. "He just had two more bottles of formula and I only have one left. I should make more bottles for him in case he wakes up hungry."

"I'll get water from the river for you."

She shook her head. "You can't take that chance. I'm sure someone will be watching the river. I don't want them to see you."

It almost sounded like she cared about his safety and not just about Paolo's supply of food. He squashed the treacherous thought and pulled her back-pack toward him. "I'll fill up all the canteens. Don't worry, no one will see me. It may take me a while, though, to run all the water through the purifier."

She held her breath for a moment, then nodded once. "Be careful." But he saw the worry in her eyes.

It was a far cry from just a few hours ago. He'd had to argue with her to convince her to wait for him. Now it was accepted that they would work together.

Don't make anything out of it, he warned himself. She was as pragmatic as he was. She knew that the baby's survival, and probably her own, depended on cooperation. There was nothing personal about it.

And he didn't want there to be. He resisted looking

back at Andi and the kid as he moved away from them. This was just a job for him, a job he was being paid for. That was all it ever would be.

Andi watched Chase disappear into the dense greenery. When she could no longer hear him, she rested her head against the tree and fought to keep her eyes open. She couldn't fall asleep. She had to pay attention, had to listen for the sounds of hunters in the jungle. She glanced down at Paolo, but he was sleeping soundly. Poor baby. He hadn't slept much as they'd walked through the jungle, and he was probably tired, too. With any luck he would sleep until Chase returned with water for his formula.

Several times she felt herself nodding off to sleep, and she jerked her head up and opened her eyes. Finally the heat and humidity combined drained away the last of her strength. Her head dropped onto her chest, and this time she didn't open her eyes.

The sound of someone moving through the jungle snapped her out of sleep, and she began to scramble to her feet. She caught herself in time, though, and lowered herself back against the tree. Paolo was still sleeping. She gently moved him so that he was behind her, hidden by the roots of the tree. Then she pulled out her gun and waited.

Whoever was out there hesitated, as if not sure which way to go. Andi gripped her gun more tightly and prayed that Paolo didn't choose now to wake up. She took a shallow breath and waited.

After a few minutes the sounds came closer. Andi didn't dare call out and ask if it was Chase. And she knew that Chase wouldn't identify himself, either. They had no way of knowing who else was in the vicinity.

With an almost silent rustling of the bushes, Chase slipped back into the tiny clearing. His gaze flickered over her gun, and she watched him tense.

Dropping down next to her, he whispered in her ear, "What's wrong?"

She shivered involuntarily as his breath danced in her ear. Her skin burned where he touched her, and she wanted to move closer to him. Instead, she edged away. "Nothing, I hope. I fell asleep and didn't wake up until I heard someone moving through the bushes. I had no idea if it was you."

He stared down at her, and she thought his green eyes darkened. Then he nodded and sat down, moving away from her. She sighed in relief. Or was it disappointment? She tried to ignore the thundering of blood in her ears.

"Go ahead and go back to sleep. We're going to be here for a while."

"Why? What did you see?"

"It's more what I *didn't* see. There was no trace of those men in the village across the river. From what I've heard of El Diablo, he doesn't give up that easily. I'm afraid they're going to start hunting through the jungle. So we're going to stay put for the time being."

"Maybe they moved on to the next village." She knew she sounded too hopeful.

"We can't afford to assume. We have to know for sure."

She nodded slowly and reluctantly. "You're right. I just feel terribly vulnerable sitting here in the open."

"That's because we *are* vulnerable." His tone was grim. "But I think we can fix that." He nodded to her left. "See that group of trees over there? Those are fig vines growing on them. The figs strangle the trees and kill them, and they die slowly from the inside out. Sometimes the center of the tree is hollow. It would give us a little more protection."

He eased away from her, and she wanted to reach out and touch him, to ask him to stay. But she curled her hands into tight fists and kept her lips pressed together. She was being foolish.

"Stay here," he whispered without looking at her. "The canteens of water are in my backpack. I've already run them through the purifier. I'll go check out the trees."

He went into the undergrowth without looking back. Andi listened intently, but she couldn't hear a thing. Chase had disappeared into the darkness like a wisp of smoke in the air, silently and without a trace.

She was being fanciful. There was nothing between her and Chase, and there couldn't be anything between them. They shared too much history, all of it bad.

Her boss had sent her to San Marcos to find a traitor, and Mac had suspected Chase and Richard. The two men had been innocent but there had been nothing innocent about the attraction that had flared between her and Chase. A week later, Richard had been killed. No, the memories they shared weren't happy ones. And they had no time for the bad ones.

She eased away from the tree and opened his pack. She might as well pass the time by making up more bottles of formula for Paolo.

When she'd finished, Chase reappeared as silently as he'd left. Squatting down next to her, he said softly, "One of the trees has a hollow base. It'll be perfect for us. Let's move over there." His breath caressed her neck, and she closed her eyes for a moment as she tried to stop herself from swaying toward him. "You take the kid, and I'll get the packs."

She swallowed once, then nodded as she forced herself to move away. It was stress, she told herself. Stress was why her hormones seemed to have gone crazy.

She busied herself with Paolo to give herself some breathing room. She was amazed that he didn't wake up when she put him into the sling, but he continued sleeping as she followed Chase through the undergrowth.

She paused once before she left the clearing to look back and make sure they hadn't left any evidence. When she turned to go, she saw that Chase had done the same thing. Their eyes met briefly, and then he nodded.

"I'll go back for a final check," he whispered. "Let's get the kid into a safe place first."

She nodded as he turned to lead the way. At least professionally they seemed to agree. Chase was cautious and careful, and Andi had to admit that, had she been by herself, she would have done very much the same as Chase was doing.

They didn't stop at the first tree that was covered with fig vines. Chase led the way through the tangled mass of vines to the center of the grove. There he pushed aside a snarl of vines to reveal a gaping hole in the bottom of the trunk.

"Have you looked inside?" she asked, hesitating.

"Yes—with my flashlight. Nothing alive in there," he answered.

Without another word she hunkered down and climbed into the tree. It was darker than El Diablo's soul, but she moved aside to make room for Chase. He eased his way in next to her, giving her a strange look.

"Don't you check places like hollow trees before you go in?" he asked.

"You said you'd checked it. I figured if there was something I needed to know about, you would have told me."

His eyes were intent on her face. "I didn't think you trusted me."

She sighed and leaned back against the wall. "We're in this together, Remington. I may not have wanted it to be this way, and I don't think you did, either, but we have no choice. If I don't trust you with small things like checking the tree before we get inside, how can I ever trust you on the big things?"

"I didn't think you would be so reasonable," he muttered.

She turned to him and gave him a tight smile. "I can be very reasonable, Remington. But I have a feeling that your definition of reasonable and mine are quite different."

His eyes flashed at her in the semidarkness of the tree, and a shiver of anticipation ran down her spine. "Oh, I think I can be very…reasonable."

His low voice scraped against her nerve endings, igniting fires everywhere. "I guess we'll see, won't we?" she murmured.

"I guess we will." In the dim light she thought she saw hot need in his eyes. Then he looked away, and the moment was gone.

"You might as well get some sleep," he said abruptly. "We're not going anywhere for a while."

Her breathing was ragged and her heart pounded in her chest. She swallowed once and looked down at Paolo, lying next to her. She had to remember what was important. "All right." Exhaustion weighted her limbs and fogged her mind. She didn't tell Chase that she'd been up most of the previous night, worrying about Paloma.

She lay down on the ground and pulled Paolo close. "Wake me up so I can take a turn watching and you can get some sleep." Her voice sounded heavy. Sleep was already overtaking her.

"All right." His voice sounded tender in the darkness, and she wondered if she was already dreaming. Then she closed her eyes and gave herself up to the bliss of sleep.

* * *

She awoke slowly, surrounded by heat and feeling completely secure. A hand was on her head, stroking her hair away from her face. The fingers were slightly calloused, and they left a trail of fire as they moved down her cheek and lingered at the angle of her jaw. Then they moved back up her face, touching her lightly as they went.

Her head rested on a hard pillow that carried Chase's scent. She felt herself smiling as she snuggled closer, then turned over. The hand on her face froze in place.

Memories came flooding back and she opened her eyes. She was supposed to be hiding in a hollow tree with Chase. She looked up and found him staring down at her.

She was lying on his lap, staring at his belt buckle. Heat washed over her face, and she scrambled to sit up.

"Take it easy," he whispered. "You'll wake the kid up."

Scooting over to the opposite side of the little cave, as far away from him as she could get, she said, "What the hell were you doing?"

"Not much," he said. "I haven't heard a thing."

"You know what I mean. What was my head doing in your lap?"

He gave her a cool smile. "Using it as a pillow. And you're welcome."

"Just tell me what's going on."

He shrugged. "You looked damned uncomfortable on the ground. So I put your head in my lap. I thought you'd sleep better." He must have noticed the panic on her face, because he gave her a taunting grin. "Was it good for you, sweetheart?"

"I didn't know you were into cheap thrills, Remington." Her heart was still thumping and her skin felt jumpy. "I hope you enjoyed it, because it's not going to happen again."

His mouth curled up in a half smile. "I'll remember you said that."

"You do that." She glanced outside, hoping he wouldn't see how much she'd been affected by waking up in his lap. "Is anything going on outside?"

His smile faded. "I haven't heard one sound that shouldn't be there."

"When do you want to leave, then?"

"It might be a while. It's getting light, and I want to make sure no one is going to be waiting for us."

"All right." It was the smart thing to do, she grudgingly admitted. She wanted to get out of the narrow confines of this tree trunk and away from Chase, but he was right. They needed to wait.

Glancing down at Paolo, she saw that he was still sleeping soundly. "He should have woken up already," she said, worry in her voice.

"He did. I gave him one of the bottles, and he fell asleep again." He looked at her defensively. "I didn't change his diaper, though. I didn't want him to wake you up."

"That was very considerate of you." Her voice softened as she looked at him and saw the weariness

in his face. "It really was. Now you should get some
sleep, too. I'm rested and I can watch."

She saw him hesitate. "Are you sure?"

"I'm positive," she said firmly. "I'll wake you if
I hear anything unusual."

He watched her for a moment, then nodded and lay
down. In moments he was asleep, his breathing slow
and even.

Andi leaned back against the trunk of the tree and
stared out into the blackness that was the jungle at
night. She wondered how Chase could tell the sun
was coming up. The curtain of vines blocked her
view, but it was so dark she wouldn't be able to see
anything, anyway. But she listened. Early morning
sounds filled the air, the low hooting of predators, the
sharp scream of prey abruptly cut off.

She wasn't sure how long she sat, listening to the
rhythm of the jungle, watching the light gradually fil-
ter through the trees, watching Chase and Paolo sleep.
Chase looked different in sleep. More approachable,
she decided. He was undeniably handsome. And since
he was sleeping, she allowed herself the luxury of
looking at him.

His wide shoulders seemed to fill the entire space.
His long legs were curled too close to her, but he
couldn't help that. She'd been studiously ignoring
their heat ever since Chase had lain down.

The hard planes of his face smoothed out in sleep,
and she saw that he had tiny lines around the corners
of his eyes. Were they laugh lines? Was Chase a man
who laughed frequently?

She hadn't thought so, but then, she didn't know him all that well. And what they did know about each other was colored with the dark brush of deception and death.

Suddenly her attention was jerked to the opening in the trunk. There were sounds coming from beyond the veil of vines that didn't belong in the jungle. The sounds of humans moving quietly through the mass of green.

She leaned over to look at Paolo. He was sound asleep, and she slowly slid him behind her, making sure he was protected.

Then she laid her hand over Chase's mouth and bent to whisper in his ear. "We have company."

He came awake instantly. She felt him nod his head, and she took her hand away from his mouth. He pulled himself to a sitting position, then his hand found her head and pulled her close.

"What did you hear?"

"People, more than one. They're moving around."

He nodded again and let her go. It seemed to Andi that his hand lingered on her neck for an instant longer than necessary, but she pushed the thought away. Chase edged closer to the opening in the base of the tree and listened intently.

Andi heard the men more clearly now. They were coming closer. Silently Chase pulled out his gun, and Andi did the same. They sat on either side of the opening, using the tree to shield them. Andi pushed Paolo farther behind her.

The men came perilously close to their hiding

place, then the sounds began to fade. Andi breathed out once and closed her eyes, then she heard a tiny sound behind her.

Paolo was awake. She saw his eyes gleam in the dim light inside the tree and heard his soft gurgling in the heavy silence.

She held her breath as she scrambled for her pack. *Please, God,* she prayed. *Don't let him start crying.*

Her hand closed around one of the bottles, and she turned and pushed it into his mouth. Her hand was shaking so badly that the nipple fell out of his mouth. She felt rather than saw him open his mouth to scream, and she shoved the nipple back in. He choked once, then gave a satisfied grunt and began sucking on the bottle.

She waited until she'd stopped shaking before scooping Paolo into her arms. Cuddling him close, she watched as his eyes began to droop. He finished the bottle and fell asleep at the same time.

After she'd carefully eased the baby back onto the ground, Chase wrapped his arm around her. "Good job," he said, his voice no more than a whisper of air. "You saved our bacon there."

Too drained to move away, as she knew she should, Andi slumped against him. "I was afraid he was going to scream again."

"He was. You got that bottle into his mouth in the nick of time." His arm tightened around her. "You saved all of us, McGinnis."

Even in the darkness she could see the intensity in

his eyes, see him watching her. And she saw the flame that leaped to life in his eyes.

He moved again, and she knew he was going to kiss her. Her heart stuttered, then began to race. Instead of moving away, as common sense told her to do, she moved closer. He touched her face gently, and she sucked in a breath. Then his mouth came down on hers.

Chapter 4

His mouth was hard and punishing, taking rather than asking. There was no gentleness, no seduction in his kiss. His mouth consumed hers, stealing what was left of her sanity.

Memories swamped her of another kiss three years ago, one that had shaken her to her very foundations. Andi had tried hard to forget that kiss. But her body hadn't forgotten a thing, and she swayed toward him.

She knew she should push him away, reestablish the boundaries between them. She had no business kissing Chase Remington. But her body betrayed her. Desire flowed hot and sharp through her veins and thickened her blood. Her skin pulsed where he touched her, and fire licked at her nerves. Instead of moving away, she kissed him back with passion and need.

She felt his hesitation, his attempt to pull away. Then with a groan he dragged her closer, spearing his hands through her hair to hold her close for his kiss. His mouth gentled on hers, and instead of bruising her lips, now he nibbled at them. He touched his tongue to the corner of her mouth, and she moaned as desire throbbed deep inside her.

When she opened her mouth, he slipped his tongue inside to taste her. She could only lock her arms around his neck and hold on as tremors shook her. His hands roamed down her back, lingering at the bottom of her spine, lightly shaping the curve of her hip.

She had to touch him. Sliding her hands beneath his shirt, she allowed herself to explore the muscles of his chest, hard and hot and slippery with sweat. She lingered in the thick hair on his chest, letting the silky strands slip through her fingers. When her fingertips brushed over his small hard nipples, he sucked in his breath and arched against her.

His hand was shaking as he bunched her T-shirt and shoved it up, then skimmed his hand over her breasts through the material of her bra. She quivered in his arms. When he pressed one finger against her nipple, she cried out and he swallowed the sound with his mouth.

She lay on his lap, his arm supporting her, his erection burning into her thigh. Her legs were trembling, and as he bent to kiss her nipple, her thighs parted for him. She heard a high-pitched moan, and recognized with a shock that the sound that had come from her.

The realization was like a dash of cold water in the face. She was sprawled all over Chase Remington, letting him touch her intimately. In a few moments she would have been begging him to make love to her.

She sat up abruptly and Chase lifted his head. "What's wrong?" His voice was harsh and guttural.

She tried to pull down her shirt, but Chase bent and took one nipple in his mouth again. Spasms of need shuddered through her, but she pushed him away.

"Stop, Chase," she said, and she despised the way her voice quavered, despised the need she heard in her words.

Slowly he sat up and stared down at her. Even in the darkness, she could see the hard glitter in his eyes, the tenseness of arousal in his face. "What's the matter?" His hand was hot and possessive as he gripped her waist.

"We can't do this." She hoped he didn't hear the desperation in her voice, didn't realize exactly how much she wanted to do this. "Look where we are!"

He continued to stare at her, and she watched as his eyes cooled. She felt the exact moment when he regained control of himself.

He set her to the side and moved as far away from her as he could get in the confined space. "You're right." His voice was flat. "It must have been temporary insanity."

She nodded, then turned away and stared out into

the dim light of dawn. She couldn't even bear to look at Chase. She didn't want him to see any hint of the turmoil inside her. "Chalk it up to stress. Is it time to leave?"

He was still breathing heavily, and her heart thundered in her chest. Her body throbbed with need, and she knew it would be a long time before she forgot what had happened here. But she forced herself to bury it deep within her heart. Chase Remington was the last man she could become involved with. Their survival, and Paolo's life, depended on their care and alertness. Every one of El Diablo's men could have walked past their hiding place in the last twenty minutes, and she would never have noticed.

"Yeah, it's time to go." Chase watched the woman silhouetted at the opening in the tree trunk and cursed steadily under his breath. He couldn't want Andi McGinnis this way, with the bone-melting all-consuming need that had taken control of his body and his mind. He tried to remind himself what she had done. He tried to conjure up an image of his dead partner. But all he could see was her face, full of passion. All he could hear were her sexy moans as he'd touched her.

Hell, he'd barely even begun to touch her and he'd been already as hot as a sixteen-year-old in the back-seat of a car with a willing girl. He'd forgotten where they were, he'd forgotten the men who searched for them, and he'd forgotten the kid who depended on them to keep their heads.

His body still ached with need, and his skin still

burned with the memory of her touch. Scowling, he tucked his shirt into his pants and practically threw himself out of the opening in the tree trunk.

"I'm going to take a look around. Stay here and get ready to move."

"Be careful." Her voice was little more than a whisper, but he heard her as he moved away.

Careful. It was too late for that. Now he knew how Andi could arouse him. He remembered what she felt like, what she tasted like. And it was far better than the forbidden memories he'd had.

He'd wanted her from the moment he'd first seen her. Even though she'd been working with him before, he hadn't been able to stay away from her. And that had been his fatal mistake.

Ever since Richard's death, he'd told himself that he couldn't still want Andi, but he couldn't prevent the dreams. Andi had haunted his sleep for years. He'd awoken countless times, hungering to touch her, wanting her taste on his lips, wondering if she would taste the same.

Now he knew. He scowled. Now he knew—but that was as far as it would go.

His body called him a liar, but he ignored the ache in his groin. He was an expert at denial. And in the next few days he wouldn't have time to worry about his body's traitorous reaction to Andi.

He forced her image out of his mind as he surveyed the jungle. There was no sign anyone else was present. Finally satisfied, he turned and headed back to the hollow tree. He found Andi sitting against the base of the tree, the backpacks on the ground and Paolo in his sling against her chest. Her face was a mask, and he couldn't tell what she was thinking.

He didn't see a trace of the turmoil that filled him. Biting back a stinging disappointment, he told himself it didn't matter. All that mattered was the job—getting her and Paolo to Monterez.

"Ready to go?" he asked. His voice was hard and cold.

She nodded as she rose to her feet. He wondered again what she was thinking, then told himself it didn't matter. He didn't want to know that much about her.

"Walk next to me until we get to the path."

She met his gaze and went still for a moment. Then she shrugged. "It'll only take a few minutes to get to the path. It'll be easier then."

"God, you are one stubborn woman." He glared at her. "You can't afford to get any more of those cuts on your face, McGinnis," he said roughly, trying to hide his emotion. "If they get infected, you're in trouble. We all are."

"All right." She avoided looking at him.

They moved through the jungle without speaking after that, although he was very aware of her presence. And she was aware of him, too, if the stiff way she held herself was any indication. He tried to ignore her, but even the overpowering smell of plants and earth couldn't mask the faint sweetness of her scent.

By the time they reached the path, his hands ached to touch her again. Unable to stop himself, he reached out and brushed her hair away from her face, using the need to look at her cuts as his excuse. There were a few new scratches, but he had been able to protect her from the majority of the branches.

"I'm fine," she said, her voice brusque as she backed away from him.

"Just checking." He hadn't missed the hitch in her breath when he'd touched her, and he tried to ignore his body's immediate response. "Is the kid all right?" he asked. "Do you need to stop and change him?"

He could see the worry in her face. "I probably should. I don't want him to get a rash in this heat and humidity. But it can wait a little longer. I want to be well away from that village before we stop."

"Good." He couldn't disguise his approval. "You've done a great job," he said gruffly.

"You sound surprised." Her eyes flashed a warning at him. "You'd better watch yourself, Remington."

Chase looked at her stiff posture and sighed. "Take it easy, McGinnis. I would have been impressed by anyone who's done what you have in the last few months. Working undercover is a tough job."

She glanced back at him, then nodded. "Sorry I jumped to conclusions."

"Why are you in this business?" he asked, and realized he was genuinely interested. "It's not an easy job, or one you'll get any credit for."

"Why did you work for the agency?" she countered coolly. "For the glory?"

"Of course not." He scowled. "It seemed like the right thing to do."

She was silent for so long that he didn't think she would answer. Finally she said, "I guess that's as good a reason as any."

His instincts told him there was more to her reasons than that, but he didn't want to pursue it. He didn't want to know anything more about Andi. He scowled. He knew far too much already, and none of it was helping him keep his distance from her.

"So we're both just damn good patriots," he muttered.

To his surprise she laughed. "I guess we are, Remington. See, we have a lot more in common than you thought."

She laughed again as she turned around and kept walking. It was only the relief at getting past the village, he told himself. That was why the sound of her laughter made him feel so giddy. That was why Andi had laughed in the first place. There was nothing more to it than that.

But he knew that wasn't true. Everything had shifted when he'd kissed her and she'd kissed him back. Now awareness hummed between them, and he knew it wouldn't go away until they'd parted. But he recognized that neither of them had any time or energy to spare for sex.

Because sex was all it would be with Andi. That was all it *could* be given their turbulent past.

The sun was high in the sky when they finally spotted the next village. As he crouched behind the trees at the edge of the river with Andi, they watched people moving around the village on the other side of the river.

"We can't take a canoe now," he whispered in her ear.

She glanced over at him, and he saw the frustration in her eyes. "I know. We're going to have to wait until tonight."

"That might be for the best." He continued to stare at the village.

"What do you mean?"

"If we grab a canoe and leave as soon as everybody is sleeping, we'll have almost the whole night to get away before they realize a canoe is missing. And we'll have a chance to eat and rest." He glanced at her face, pinched with fatigue. "Don't worry, we'll still get to Monterez in time."

She turned to look at him. "Yes, we will. Because we have to." She gave him a strained smile. "But you're right. We have to eat and rest. Let's go look for someplace to hide."

He saw the effort it cost her to stop and rest. "You need to tell me what your information is," he said quietly. "Anything that important shouldn't be entrusted to only one person. I need to know, in case…"

He stumbled over the words, but she nodded. "You're right. I'll tell you everything Paloma told me as soon as we have a chance."

She spoke coolly and dispassionately, and he felt another surge of appreciation for her skill and dedication. He'd never known a woman quite like her, a woman so dedicated to her job that she could contemplate her own death with such calmness. He'd never been *involved* with a woman like her before.

And he didn't intend to start now. After leading her through the jungle, he finally found a hidden hollow at the base of a huge liana tree. The roots jutted out like buttresses in front of it, making a spot where they would be concealed.

"This will work." He watched her place Paolo carefully on the ground, but busied himself with his pack so he wouldn't see the way her hand lingered over the baby.

"We need to eat. Do you have anything in your pack?"

"I have enough meals for myself," she said, not looking at him, either. As he sat between the roots of the huge tree, too close to Andi, his body hummed with awareness. He wondered if hers did, too. "How about you?"

"I have plenty of food. I figured I'd have Paloma and Paolo back in the city in about three hours, but I always pack like it could be a couple of weeks." He reached into his knapsack and pulled out the first thing he touched—a foil-wrapped dehydrated meal for two. "Use the water in the canteens to rehydrate it. I'll get more water as soon as we're finished."

They ate the cold unappetizing food in an uneasy silence, neither of them looking at the other. Andi tended to Paolo's needs as soon as they were finished, and Chase gathered up their canteens and all the dirty diapers and headed for the river.

When he returned to the liana tree, he saw Andi giving Paolo another bottle. He squatted down next to them, looking at the contented baby with unwilling fascination.

"He's hardly cried at all since we've been on the move. Isn't that unusual?"

She tilted her head and watched the baby for a moment. "It is a little unlike Paolo. He's always been very ready to let me know if he's unhappy. I do know that we're being very attentive to him and feeding him whenever he looks like he might cry. So it may be just the regular meals that're keeping him happy."

"*You're* the one who's been taking care of him," he said gruffly. "I guess I should thank you."

"No thanks are required." Her voice was stiff. "I love Paolo. Taking care of him isn't a burden. And anyone would have done the same thing under the circumstances."

"Not everyone, McGinnis," he said quietly. "A lot of agents wouldn't have risked their lives like this, even for a baby."

She looked up at him. "Given the choice, would you have risked taking Paolo with you?"

He only hesitated for a moment. "I like to think I would have. But I've never had to make that choice." He paused, then added, "And even this time the choice was made for me."

"I told you that you had no obligation to help us."

She looked down at the baby, and the expression on her face was one of fierce protectiveness.

He watched them for a moment and realized that he hadn't had a choice, not from the very beginning. Job or no job, money or no money, he couldn't have left the baby in that town, knowing that men would be coming to kill him. And he couldn't have left Andi behind, either.

Chapter 5

Andi sat in the bottom of the canoe, holding onto Paolo and watching Chase expertly paddle the tiny craft. After sleeping most of the day, Chase had tracked down the crude craft and then brought them to where he'd anchored it downstream. His shoulder muscles rippled and bunched beneath his shirt as he stroked first on one side of the canoe, then the other.

The baby had drifted off to sleep shortly after they'd started down the river. The total darkness of the jungle pressed in on them, and Andi could see nothing but Chase, sitting in front of her. Watching him was making her nerves jump and her stomach flutter. She tried to focus on her job, but here in the darkness, with Chase so close, it was hard to ignore him. She almost wished Paolo would wake up—anything to offer a distraction.

Suddenly Chase stopped paddling and leaned toward her. "It's too dark to get a good look at my map," he said in a low whisper. "Do you know where the next village is along the river?"

"We should be getting to it soon," she answered, trying not to notice the way his arm brushed against her leg. "It's about five miles from the last village. We've gone about that far now, haven't we?"

He shifted his weight. "I think so." He gestured at Paolo. "How's he doing?"

"Still sleeping." She raised the bottle she was holding. "And I'm ready when he wakes up."

"Good."

It was just one word, tossed at her in the most casual way possible, but it made her glow. She scowled at the river. He shouldn't have that much power over her. A single word from him shouldn't make her melt inside.

The canoe was starting to drift toward the bank, so Chase resumed paddling. Again she found herself staring at the play of his muscles, and she deliberately turned her gaze away.

Chase's voice came out of the darkness. "Do you think you can get off the seat and down into the bottom of the canoe with him?"

"Sure," she said. "What do you have in mind?"

"I want you hidden when we go past the next village, just in case someone is watching."

"What about you?" She stared at him, her heart suddenly pounding. The darkness had lent a false sense of security, as if they were invisible while gliding silently down the river. Chase's reminder brought reality crashing back.

"I'm going to sit on the bottom of the boat, too, then I'll bend way over while I paddle. We won't move as quickly, but there's less chance we'll be seen if we keep low."

After a few moments Chase ceased stroking again. "The village is coming up," he whispered, and Andi saw a faint break in the total darkness of the jungle at night. "Get down."

She slid off the seat and onto the floor of the canoe. It rocked slightly, but Chase held it steady with his paddle. Paolo gave a start from the sudden movement, then relaxed again.

Chase looked at them and nodded. Then he looked at the approaching village and his mouth hardened. "Do you have your gun handy?"

"Yes."

"Don't hesitate to use it."

"Don't worry, I'll be ready."

To her surprise he flashed her a quick smile. "I know you will."

Why did she feel as if she'd just been given the moon and stars on a platter? Damn! She didn't care about his opinion of her, she told herself fiercely.

She watched as Chase slid to the floor and bent himself nearly double. He continued to paddle steadily and silently, but his cramped position made it difficult and the canoe slowed down.

Suddenly he froze, his paddle suspended just above

the surface of the water. At the same time she heard the low murmur of male voices drift across the water.

She turned her head away from the village so that her pale face wouldn't give them away in the darkness. Now she couldn't see what was happening, but she rested her hand on the butt of her gun.

Chase didn't move, and she knew the canoe must be drifting toward the bank of the river opposite the village. She strained to hear the voices, to distinguish the words. Just then the men on the riverbank laughed loudly, and she saw Chase dip the paddle into the water and pull as hard as he could.

"Hold on and keep low." His whisper was harsh. "Those two men must be El Diablo's. They think this is a log floating down the river. They're talking about doing some target practice."

Chase had barely finished speaking when two gunshots cracked the silence of the night. Andi heard the whine of the bullets as they went over her head, smelled the acrid odor of gunpowder drifting across the water.

Chase cursed low and long and stroked even harder.

"Can I help paddle?" she whispered.

"No. Just stay down."

She checked to make sure that Paolo was completely protected by her body, then tried to force herself lower in the hull. The two men laughed again, and she again strained to hear their words. Chase apparently heard, because he began to pull even harder on the paddle.

Two more shots rang out, and this time the canoe rocked wildly to the side. "Chase!" she hissed. "Are you all right?"

"I'm fine, but the canoe was hit." His voice was grim. "We're taking in water."

As he spoke, Andi felt water seeping through the material of her pants. She lifted Paolo against her chest as the water crept steadily higher. In a few minutes the canoe sat noticeably lower in the water. "We're going to have to stop."

"I want to get as far away from the village as possible."

He continued to paddle, his strokes long and hard. Finally, when the water was threatening to sink the canoe, he headed for the shore.

Chase jumped out of the canoe and dragged it onto the riverbank, then Andi handed him the baby. Chase set Paolo on the ground, then helped Andi out of the canoe. He put his hands on her waist to steady her.

Grasping his arms, she asked, "Are you sure you're all right?"

His hands tightened on her waist. "I'm fine. How about you?"

"I'm only wet." She looked up into his face, barely visible in the moonlight, and stepped closer to him. "When the canoe jerked so sharply, I was afraid you'd been hit."

"I was afraid it was you." He closed his eyes and pulled her hard against his body. "It took everything I had to keep paddling."

Her heart pounded and her blood raced. His musky

masculine scent surrounded her, and the length of his body burned into hers. Her skin jumped where he held her.

She told herself to move away from him, but she couldn't think. She could only feel. And nothing felt more right than being in Chase's arms. Nothing felt more natural than leaning against him and soaking in his strength and his warmth.

When he bent his head toward her, she didn't think at all. She simply lifted her face and met his lips. He took her mouth like a starving man given a feast, and she leaned into him. He groaned when their mouths met, and her head began to spin.

She tried to speak, but all the air was trapped in her chest. She couldn't breathe, couldn't think. All she could do was feel. Chase trailed his hand down her back, pausing at each bump on her spine, touching her as if she was precious and fragile. When she moved, trying to get closer to him, he groaned again before pulling her into the V of his legs and moving intimately against her. She felt his erection against her abdomen and knew she should move away. But instead, she pressed closer.

He trailed his lips over her face, pausing at the angle of her jaw, then moved down her neck. Desire throbbed heavily inside her. Suddenly the world tilted, and she realized that Chase had picked her up. He laid her down in the grass that lined the riverbank, then stretched out beside her.

He eased one leg between her thighs, and she wrapped herself around him, trying to pull him closer.

He groaned again, deep in his throat, and shoved her T-shirt up over her chest.

When his hand closed over her breast, she heard herself cry out. Frantically she pulled his mouth to hers again, losing herself in his kiss. Nothing existed but Chase and the trembling demands of her body. When he bent his head to take her nipple into his mouth, she cried out again. Her hands shook as she held his head to her breast.

She heard the sound, but it didn't register. It couldn't break through the sensual haze that held her in its grip. Then the noise came again, sharper this time, and Chase raised his head.

She gripped his arms, aching to feel his mouth on her again, her body aroused and throbbing. Then she recognized the beginning of a wail from Paolo, awake now and hungry.

She scrambled to sit up, and Chase moved to the side. She didn't look at him as she pulled her shirt down over her aching breasts. She couldn't force herself to meet his gaze as she reached for the baby.

Paolo stared up at her, his eyes wide in the faint moonlight, and she saw him draw in a breath for one of his ear-shattering screams.

She turned to her backpack to grab a bottle of formula, but Chase had already done so. Silently he handed her a bottle, and she mumbled her thanks. Without looking at him, she rested against a tree and fed Paolo.

The sucking sounds coming from Paolo seemed to fill the air around her, drowning out the frantic beating of her heart. She could feel Chase's gaze on her, but she busied herself with Paolo. Finally, when he had almost finished the bottle and his eyes began to close, she looked up at Chase.

He was staring at her, but when their eyes met, he stood up. "I'm going to take a look at the canoe," he said, his voice gruff.

"Good," she said, her voice equally strained.

Apparently they were going to pretend that the passionate embrace had never happened. That was fine with her, because it shouldn't have ever happened. And if she hadn't been so frantic with fear for Chase, it wouldn't have.

Chase turned away from Andi as she changed Paolo's diaper, giving fervent thanks for the concealing darkness. He was too unsettled, too off balance, to face Andi right now.

Why the hell had he kissed her? And why had she kissed him back? They didn't even like each other. He jerked the canoe farther onto the riverbank and wedged it against a tree.

His body liked her just fine, he thought sourly as he took out his flashlight and examined the hole in the hull of the canoe. That was the problem.

"How does it look?" Andi stood next to him, holding Paolo against her shoulder. Her face was pinched with worry, and all traces of passion had disappeared.

That was what he wanted, he told himself. He wanted nothing but business between them. "It looks like we came damn close to buying the farm," he said, scowling at her.

Panic flashed in her eyes as she moved to look more closely at the hole. "Maybe we can fix it."

"Yeah, I'll pull out my handy fix-a-canoe kit, and we'll set off again in no time."

She stood up straight and glared at him. "Sarcasm isn't going to solve anything. If it's really beyond repair, I'll start walking to Monterez right now. But I think we should at least try to repair it. We only have three more days to get to Monterez."

A lock of hair fell into her face, making her look like a bedraggled waif, but her eyes were fierce with determination. He sighed and couldn't stop himself from brushing the hair back. "I'm sorry, McGinnis. I didn't mean to snap at you." His fingers lingered at her jaw, then fell away. "I'll make a plug for the hole. It won't work perfectly, but it should last long enough for us to get farther down the river."

She hadn't moved away when he touched her. She stood staring at him, her eyes wide, looking more vulnerable than he'd ever seen her. His heart moved in his chest and he almost reached out and pulled her close. Then she blinked and backed up a step. "What can I do to help?"

"Watch the kid," he said gruffly.

"Paolo is asleep again." She set him down carefully in the space between two trees, then turned to him. "It'll go faster with two people working on the boat."

"Suit yourself." He needed some distraction, he thought desperately. He didn't want to stand here, looking at Andi in the moonlight. "You never did tell me why we're in such a rush to get to Monterez."

"We haven't had time," she said.

"We've got a lot of time now." He found a hatchet in his backpack, then shone the beam of the flashlight on the surrounding trees, looking for the right kind of wood. "Why don't you fill me in?"

She hesitated for too long, and he finally swung around to face her. "Or don't you trust me with your information?"

"Of course I trust you," she said immediately. "I'm just trying to figure out how much you want to hear."

"Tell me everything," he said as he selected a strong wiry sapling and began to chop it down. "It'll be easier to make decisions if we both have the same information." He refused to admit that he suddenly wanted to know everything that had happened to her in the past few months. It was merely business, he told himself.

"All right."

She moved behind him and reached out to hold the sapling steady as he chopped. Once again, their unspoken communication made him uneasy, but he ignored the feeling. "You've told me the bare bones already, but start at the beginning."

"I got to Chipultipe about two months ago. That was two months after Paloma had first made contact with the agency. Her husband had been killed a few months earlier, and she'd just given birth to Paolo. The agency promised to take care of both of them.

We were fortunate in the timing, because the village had requested a teacher from the Peace Corps about a year earlier. So no one was suspicious when I showed up.''

"How did you make contact with Paloma?"

"I knew who she was and where she lived. I waited until I'd been in the village for a week or so, then I went to her house very late one night. I woke her up and told her who I was. We worked out the details that night, and a few days later she made up an excuse to ask me to watch Paolo for her. I acted reluctant at first, but finally gave in. So she had a reason for seeing me every day.''

"You had a nice little setup." She had done a great job, he realized. She'd managed to get into the village without suspicion, then to think of a reason to see her source every day.

"It worked well," she agreed. "Maybe too well. I don't know what happened, why El Diablo got suspicious of Paloma. And maybe nothing happened. Maybe he just heard that a foreigner was watching Paolo and didn't like it. I don't think anyone else in the village suspected who I was. I was really careful never to ask any questions about El Diablo, never to appear to be anything more than a teacher.''

"Don't beat yourself up," he said, setting the hatchet on the ground and turning to her. "You can't control everything when you're undercover." His face darkened. "I learned the hard way."

"I know." Her voice was low and passionate. "I've told myself that over and over. But Paloma still died. And if I hadn't gone to the village, she'd still be alive.''

"Maybe, maybe not." Andi was too tempting, standing so close to him, the agony of what had happened to Paolo's mother vivid on her face. He picked up the hatchet and turned away. "Criminals like El Diablo don't thrive and get stronger because they're humanitarians. Chances are, Paloma would have gotten killed eventually, anyway. People who work for criminals like him tend to have short life spans.''

"She was just a maid!" Andi said passionately. "He would have no reason to kill her."

"Men like El Diablo don't need a reason to kill." Chase took a violent swing at the tree. "Maids are in a position to see and hear an awful lot. Maybe he killed his maids regularly, after they'd been working for him awhile. How do you know?''

There was a long pause behind him. "It's kind of you to try and make me feel less guilty," she finally said, her voice quiet. "I appreciate the thought. But that's not the issue. The issue is the information Paloma gave me.''

The sapling finally cracked and fell, and Chase pulled it into the small clearing. "Here, hold the flashlight while I cut out two plugs.''

Andi took the flashlight and trained it steadily on the tree. "Paloma told me she'd heard El Diablo talking about a meeting he was going to have. She told me the names of the men, but they didn't mean anything to her.''

"But they did to you," he said.

She nodded. "They were the heads of two of the biggest drug cartels in South America. As soon as I heard about the meeting, I knew we had to stop it. If El Diablo, the most powerful drug dealer in Central America, hooked up with those two men, the three of them could create a huge and almost unstoppable conglomerate. They would be able to move drugs around the world with impunity."

"Paloma didn't know when this meeting was supposed to take place?"

"No." Andi tightened her lips. "But I asked her to keep her ears open to see if she could find out. I'm afraid she might have taken too many chances, done something careless and made El Diablo realize she was spying on him."

Chase put the sapling aside and took both her hands. "Her death was not your fault, Andi." Her name felt too intimate on his lips, far more intimate than McGinnis. "Informers know how dangerous their job is, and they choose to do it, anyway. We'll never completely know why. We can mourn them, but we can't let ourselves be swamped by guilt when they're killed. It just gets in the way of doing our jobs."

"I know." She turned her hands so they were gripping his and twined their fingers together. Chase felt his heart jump. "And thank you for telling me, again, what I should know. But every time I look at Paolo, all I can see is a child who will never know his mother. And I can't help but feel responsible."

He held her hands for a moment longer, allowing

himself the pleasure, knowing that it comforted her. Then he drew his hands away. The only thing that would help Andi right now was getting the canoe fixed.

"What did she tell you when she came to your house that last night?"

Andi folded her hands in her lap and stared into the night. "She was almost dead when she got there. She could barely speak. But she asked me to take care of Paolo, told me to pack his things in her blue backpack and get out of the village. She was afraid El Diablo would try to kill him, too."

She took a deep trembling breath. "And she told me she had heard the time and place of the meeting. It was in five days, at an abandoned airstrip in the middle of the jungle, about an hour away from Monterez. The two men from South America were going to fly in, stay for just a short time, then fly out. There would be other meetings later to cement the deal."

"The first thing you should have done was get your radio and pass on the information."

"Paolo had to come first," she said immediately. "His life was more important than passing on the information. I was going to stop for the radio on our way out of the village. Then you showed up and everything went to hell."

"We could have gone back for your radio."

Andi shook her head. "I thought of that, but I wasn't willing to risk his life. Paloma died to get me that information, and I intend to make sure that El Diablo is captured. But it's not worth Paolo's life."

Chase held up one of the plugs of wood he'd whittled out of the sapling. "Then let's see if we can jam this into the hole in the canoe. We don't have time to waste."

Andi scrambled up and held the flashlight steadily on the hole while he used the side of the hatchet blade to pound in the plugs. Then he stood back and examined the canoe.

"It's not perfect, but I think they'll do the trick." He glanced up at the sky, then looked at his watch. "We still have a few more hours of darkness. Let's see how much farther we can get."

Andi immediately hoisted her backpack onto her shoulders. "I don't know this part of San Marcos very well. How far are we going to take the river?"

"This part of the jungle is pretty much uninhabited, it seems. I've looked at the map, and it appears we could take the river all the way into Monterez, but I think that would be too dangerous. The closer we get to the capital, the more traffic there'll be on the river and the more we'll stand out. We'll take it as far as we can, but at some point we'll have to leave the canoe behind and find another way into the city."

"El Diablo isn't going to give up looking for me. I'm sure by now he's figured out that I was Paloma's contact, if only because I disappeared with Paolo."

"I'm sure he has. But the farther we get away from Chipultipe, the better our chances. It forces him to search a bigger area. With a little bit of luck, we'll be able to sneak into Monterez before he knows we're there."

"All right."

He turned to look at her. "You're agreeing that easily?"

Andi looked at him directly. "I already told you that I don't know San Marcos as well as you do. If I didn't trust your judgment, Remington, I wouldn't have left Chipultipe with you. We're not going to make it to Monterez if we fight over everything."

"Andi McGinnis agreeing with me. I guess miracles do happen."

"I don't know about miracles, but I can guarantee you'll be seeing visions if you don't watch your mouth." She gave him a sweet smile as she picked up Paolo. "I figure you don't want to be killed any more than I do. And since you're the expert on San Marcos, I'm willing to let you make the decisions here."

"I'm touched."

Her smile faded and she sighed. "Look, Remington, our past history isn't that great, and I'll be the first to admit it. But I know you're a good agent, one of the best. And I trust you to get Paolo safely to Monterez. So let's get going."

Chase stared at her for a moment. Andi McGinnis had just placed her life, and Paolo's, in his hands. He felt like he'd been gut-punched.

Chapter 6

"Tell me about your business." Andi's voice cut through the darkness, and she saw Chase stop paddling for a fraction of a second, then resume.

"Why do you want to know?"

She shrugged. "Just curious, I guess. We have to pass the time somehow."

"So we play twenty questions?"

"Forget it," she said stiffly. "I was trying to make conversation, but I can see I shouldn't have bothered. Forgive me for prying."

He sighed. "Look, McGinnis, I'm sorry. I'm not much for the social graces."

"I wasn't asking for graceful," she snapped. "I'd settle for civil."

He waited a beat, then said, "All right, civil it is. What do you want to know about me?"

She wanted to know everything, she realized, and alarm bells went off in her brain. She couldn't be interested in Chase Remington. Sure, her body hummed when he was close, and his kisses melted her socks, but that was only physical. Just adrenaline and proximity.

She and Chase were far too different. They wanted different things out of life. She wasn't interested in tying herself to a man, especially a man like Chase. He was too domineering, too strong. She wasn't about to surrender her hard-won independence to any man.

But she could carry on a conversation with him, she told herself. They had to do *something* to pass the time.

Chase's kisses, the way his hands felt on her body filled her head, but she firmly pushed the memories away. *That* wasn't how they were going to pass the time.

"What kind of business do you have?" she asked, instead, trying to ignore the breathlessness of her voice.

He hesitated a moment. Finally he said, "I have a private-investigation and security business in Denver."

"That's how Mac got you down here? He hired you?"

He nodded, and she saw his anger in the stiffening of his posture. "I had no idea it was Mac. Some guy I'd never met called and said he wanted me to go to Chipultipe. I said no thanks, because I didn't want to come back to San Marcos. But he made me an offer I couldn't refuse, as they say.''

''What was that?''

''Money,'' he said bluntly. ''My business is growing, and I want to expand. But to do that, I need a chunk of money. With what this guy was going to pay me I could hire an associate and get more office space.''

''Weren't you a little suspicious that he was willing to pay you so much for such a simple job?''

''I suppose I was, but I told myself he was rich and desperate. The job sounded easy enough, and I really needed the money. I figured it couldn't be that tough to escort a woman and her kid to the capital city.''

''Famous last words, Remington?''

''Nah.'' He turned around and gave her a grin. It was the first time she'd seen him smile, and her breath caught in her chest. ''So far it's been a piece of cake.''

''Yep, it's been a real Sunday stroll in the park.'' Paolo stirred on her lap, and she looked down at him anxiously.

''Is he all right?'' Chase asked.

Andi looked at him, startled. ''Why do you think he's not?''

Chase shrugged. ''He's been moving around a lot. He doesn't usually do that when he sleeps.''

''You're right.'' She stared at him. ''That's very observant of you. I didn't think you paid that much attention to Paolo.''

He shrugged again. "He's the wild card in this out-fit. We can't control what he does, but it affects us big-time. I have to pay attention to him."

His voice was offhand, but he turned around again and looked at the baby. Andi could see the concern in his eyes. It made her soften inside.

"Remington, you are a big fraud," she said with a smile. "You're nuts about him, aren't you?"

Chase scowled. "He's a kid and kids are cute. What's not to like?"

Her laugh bubbled out of her throat. "He's got you wrapped around his little finger, hasn't he?"

"Cut it out, McGinnis. Just make sure he's all right."

Her smile faded as she looked down at Paolo again. He was still sleeping, but he was indeed moving rest-lessly. "I don't know," she said. "And every once in a while he whimpers in his sleep."

"My dog does that sometimes. Maybe he's just dreaming."

In spite of her worry, she had to stifle a snort of laughter. "He's not a dog, Remington. He's a baby."

"Who says babies can't dream?"

"I'm sure they can. But I don't remember him act-ing like this before."

"Do you want to stop?"

Andi looked down at the sleeping Paolo for a mo-ment and wondered if they should. She *was* worried about him. "No," she finally said. "We need to make up the time we spent plugging the hole."

"All right."

The canoe slipped silently through the darkness, and Andi brushed a hand over Paolo's downy hair. His mouth pursed in his sleep, and he let out another whimper. She wondered if he was getting hungry again. As she was reaching for a bottle from the backpack, he opened his eyes and stared at her.

Picking him up, she cuddled him in the curve of her arm and offered him the bottle. After one taste he turned his head away. Andi nuzzled his neck and murmured, "What's the matter, sweetie? Are you just restless like Chase and me?"

Paolo gave a short fretful cry, then reached for Andi's face. But instead of smiling and gurgling like he usually did, he cried out again. Andi shifted him so that he was resting against her shoulder and patted his back. After squirming for a few minutes he belched, then seemed to settle down.

"How's he doing?" Chase asked.

"Well, he didn't want to eat and he's still restless. I'm afraid something's wrong, but I don't know what."

At that moment Paolo let out a piercing scream and his tiny body went rigid. As Andi patted his back, his muscles finally relaxed, but he began sobbing.

"I think we need to stop," Andi said to Chase. "I need to find out what's wrong with him."

Chase turned the canoe toward the riverbank and, reaching for the rope, quickly secured it to a tree that hung over the water. Then he jumped out and reached for Paolo.

Andi handed him the baby and watched as he

tucked the infant carefully into the crook of one arm. Then he extended his hand to Andi and helped her out of the canoe.

"Let's get a look at him," Chase murmured. He nodded at his backpack. "My flashlight should be right on top."

Andi found the flashlight, then took a blanket out of her pack. She spread it on the ground, then waited for Chase to lay Paolo on top of it.

He seemed reluctant to put the baby down, but he finally set him gently on the ground. Andi trained her flashlight on Paolo, being careful not to shine the light in his eyes.

There were tears on his cheeks, but she didn't notice anything else unusual. She laid a hand on his forehead. "He doesn't feel feverish," she said after a moment.

"Maybe he has some insect bites," Chase suggested.

"Let's look."

They lifted his shirt and examined his tender skin, but they didn't see any bites. "I'll check his diaper," Andi said.

A few moments later she rocked back on her heels. "That's the problem," she said. "He has diarrhea. He's probably got cramps. No wonder he's been restless."

"Why would he have diarrhea?" Chase leaned over the baby, frowning with concern.

"Because I haven't heated the water for his formula," she answered grimly. "I worried about it, but

I knew we couldn't take the chance on building a fire when we were so close to the village. I was afraid it would give us away. So I just gave him the formula without boiling the water.''

"I put the water through the purifier." Chase looked up at her and she saw the worry in his eyes.

"I know. And that works fine for us, but I guess not for an infant." She picked Paolo up and held him closely. "Poor baby. No wonder you've been restless."

"What can we do for him?"

"We can start by heating the water we use to mix his formula."

"We'd still be taking a chance if we build a fire at night," Chase said.

Andi rubbed Paolo's back and was pleased when he belched again. "Then I guess we'll have to wait until daylight. I've changed his diaper. I don't think he's going to want to eat much right now, anyway."

"I have some diarrhea medicine in my first-aid kit," Chase said. "Should we give him some of that?"

Andi stared at him, unsure. "I don't know. It's medicine for adults."

Before Chase could answer, Paolo began to cry again. His painful hiccuping sobs tore at her heart. Finally she said, "Let's give him just a little and see what happens."

Chase tore through his pack and finally pulled out the first-aid box. Opening it up, he took out a bottle of liquid medicine and held the flashlight on the directions.

"This says to give an adult two to three teaspoons, three times a day." He looked up at her. "So how much should we give a baby?"

"Maybe just a few drops." Andi glanced down at Paolo, fear churning in her stomach. "We can always give him more."

"All right." Chase put the flashlight on the ground and held the bottle. "How should I do this?"

"Pour a few drops into the cap, and I'll dribble it into his mouth."

She watched Chase carefully measure out a few drops of the medicine and realized his hands were shaking. He was just as scared for Paolo as she was. Even through her worry, her heart warmed at the thought.

Paolo choked and cried when she dropped the medicine into his mouth, but she rubbed his back and murmured to him, and he finally calmed down. She and Chase sat on the bank of the river watching him until his eyes drooped and he fell asleep.

"Is he all right? Should he fall asleep like that?" Chase asked, leaning over to look at Paolo.

"I have no idea. But if he's sleeping, he can't be in pain."

Chase looked up at her. "What do you want to do? Should we wait here and see what happens? Or do you want to get back into the canoe and continue down the river?"

"What do you think?" Andi asked.

"As long as he's sleeping, I think we should keep moving," Chase replied. "We can stop again when he wakes up. But there's really no reason to stay here if he's going to sleep for a while."

"You're right. Let's go."

They continued down the river as the sun rose. Before long, its heat beat down on them, and sweat poured off Chase. Andi could see he was tiring. He kept up his steady strokes of the paddle, but they weren't moving as fast.

"Why don't you let me take a turn paddling the canoe?" she said. "You can hold Paolo for a while."

"I'm stronger than you, McGinnis. It makes more sense for me to paddle."

"I know you're stronger, but you've been paddling all night. You need to rest."

He met her gaze. "McGinnis, it doesn't make any sense for you to paddle the canoe. That's not using our resources to the maximum."

"Our resources won't do us a damn bit of good if they collapse from exhaustion," she said as she leaned forward and handed him the sleeping Paolo. He took the baby automatically and she grabbed the paddle. "I'll do this while you rest for a while and eat something."

He stared at her for a moment, then looked down at the baby. "You always were a bossy one, McGinnis," he murmured. But he didn't sound angry.

"You haven't seen bossy yet, Remington," she retorted. "You lose the paddle because you're too tired to hang on to it, and you'll find out just how bossy I can be.''

"I'm shaking with fear."

"You're a smart man."

After a few moments Chase rummaged in his pack and pulled out a packet of freeze-dried food, then dumped some of the water from his canteen into it. When he'd finished eating, he looked at her and said quietly, "Thank you, Andi."

She felt her face heating. "What for? Bossing you around?"

He studied her for a moment, then gave a half grin. "Among other things. Everyone needs some bossing around once in a while."

"You're welcome," she said, almost stumbling on the words. She didn't really want to see that light in Chase's eyes. She didn't really want to feel his approval—and bask in it.

She needed to change the subject and she needed to do it now, before she made a total fool of herself. She looked away and nodded at the jungle that pressed so close to the river. "I haven't seen a sign of anyone since it got light."

His eyes shifted, but not before she saw what could have been a flicker of disappointment in them. "With any luck we won't see a soul for a long time."

He shifted on the hard seat of the canoe, but held Paolo carefully against his body. She noticed that he hadn't set the baby on his lap once. He'd held the infant in his arms ever since she handed Paolo to him.

"I'll just keep going, then."

"I can take over again," he said.

She shook her head. "I'm fine. It feels good to do something after sitting still all night."

"Yeah, you've been doing nothing but sitting around and eating chocolates for the past two days. You sure do need the exercise."

She grinned. "I'm glad you understand."

They moved along for the next hour as the sun rose steadily higher in the sky. Andi's arms were tiring, but she'd die before she admitted that to Chase. He'd been murmuring in a low voice to Paolo, and when she wasn't scanning the jungle, Andi watched them.

Paolo, awake now, began kicking his legs and waving his arms, his gaze on Chase, and pretty soon Andi could hear the baby giggling. She saw that Chase was making faces at him. Paolo was delighted.

Chase eventually turned around and said, "He's getting pretty lively. Do you think we should stop?"

"I don't want to stop, but we probably should." She kept paddling, although her arms felt leaden. "I'll keep my eye open for a good spot."

In another fifteen minutes she saw a small clearing on the edge of the river, large enough to pull the canoe ashore. She paddled toward it.

As they reached the bank, Chase turned around and handed Paolo to her. Then he jumped out and pulled the front end of the canoe onto the bank. He reached for Paolo, and Andi realized that her arms were shaking as she handed him the baby.

After setting Paolo on the ground, Chase turned back to Andi, lifting her out of the boat. She thought his hands lingered at her waist for moments longer than they needed to, then he let her go and pulled the canoe all the way onto the shore.

"Why don't you stay here with Paolo for a few minutes? I'm going to take a look behind us and find a spot to rest. I'd rather not be in full view of anyone going down the river. We haven't seen a soul, and I'd like to keep it that way."

She nodded, too exhausted to answer. Chase disappeared into the brush, and she turned to Paolo.

"How are you doing, big guy?" she crooned as she bent over him. She tried to pick him up, but her arms still shook too badly. She could manage a diaper change, though, and as she worked, he beamed at her. "I think you are feeling better," she said. "Wait until Chase hears that."

"Wait until I hear what?"

She spun around to see Chase standing behind her. "I didn't hear you.'

"I know. You were just too busy with junior."

"I think he's feeling a little better. That medicine must have helped."

"Should we give him more?"

She nodded. "A little, perhaps."

He filled the cap of the bottle and handed it to her. But her hands were still shaking so much that she couldn't get the cap close to Paolo's mouth. After a moment she felt Chase's hands on hers. "Let me do it."

He set the capful of medicine on the ground, then picked Paolo up. More gently than she could have imagined, he bent over the baby and got him to open his mouth. Chase then dribbled the medicine in, patting Paolo's back while he swallowed.

"You do that like a pro," she murmured, touched at Chase's gentleness with the baby.

He shrugged. "I just watched you last time."

He kept Paolo in his arms, rocking him almost absently. "Your arms are still trembling from all that paddling."

Andi looked at her hands, then hid them behind her back. "I'm fine. Are we ready to leave?"

Chase continued to rock Paolo. "Not yet. I think we need to heat some water and eat something as long as we're stopped."

"All right." She looked around for firewood. "Where do you want to build a fire?"

"We don't have to do that. I have a small stove in my pack."

Andi stopped and stared at him. "Why would you bring a stove for what you thought was going to be a simple trip by car?"

"I'm always prepared, McGinnis." His face hardened. "I learned when I was working for Mac that if something can go wrong, it will. So I think of everything that can go wrong on a job, then add ten more things. And I make sure I have everything I need for all those problems."

But he hadn't had anything in his pack to save his partner from being killed, Andi thought. Nothing could have prevented Richard's death. She wondered if he was thinking the same thing. From the forbidding look on his face, she suspected he was.

"I'm glad," she said quietly. "It'll be a lot easier than trying to start a fire."

The hardness on his face eased. "Why don't you take the kid and I'll start heating some water."

Andi took Paolo out of his arms. The baby's eyelids were starting to droop again, and she wondered if the medicine made him sleepy.

"I'm sorry if I brought up painful memories," she said quietly. "I didn't think."

"Don't worry about it." His face closed again. "I don't intend to."

Chase scowled as he watched Andi murmur to Paolo. It was a damn good thing she'd made him remember what had happened with Richard. He'd almost forgotten the lesson Richard's death had taught him—never get involved with someone you're working with.

Andi was dangerous. She made him forget the rules, forget lessons he'd learned too early in life. He'd survived for thirty years by trusting no one, and he didn't intend to change his habits now.

He deliberately turned away as she crooned to the baby. Sure, it made his heart twist in his chest to look at her with the kid. Hell, he'd already more than half fallen for Paolo himself. But Paolo didn't count. He was just a baby, and babies couldn't let you down. He was safe. And he wouldn't see the kid after Monterez, anyway.

That made him wonder what was going to happen

to Paolo, and he scowled again. He didn't care. There were all kinds of agencies to handle things like that. It wasn't any of his business.

He stomped down to the river to gather water and waited while it ran through the purifier, trying to put the image of Paolo alone and afraid out of his mind. He busied himself by watching the river and the surrounding area, watching for signs of human presence. When he'd filled his canteen, he poured the water into the small pan that sat on top of the stove and waited for the water to boil.

It took an hour to boil a sufficient quantity. Finally, when everything was stowed away in their packs and the canoe was hidden from sight, he knew he had to get some sleep. Both he and Andi had been running on adrenaline since they'd left Chipultipe, but they were going to crash soon if they didn't take care of themselves. He pulled a package of mosquito netting out of his pack, then lay down next to Andi and Paolo. After covering the three of them with the netting, he allowed himself to fall asleep.

Chapter 7

Chase awoke slowly, surrounded by Andi's scent. His body ached for her so badly that he imagined she filled his arms. His hands tightened on her. He wanted to hold on to the dream for as long as possible.

A tiny sound, almost like a moan, cut through the haze of sleep. There was a hand pressed to his chest, and he knew it was only a dream, but he kept his eyes closed. He didn't want to wake up, didn't want to face the world just yet. He wanted to savor the fantasy of Andi touching him for just a while longer.

Then someone moaned again, and the hand moved on his chest. He opened his eyes to find that Andi was curled into him, sound asleep. She'd fisted her hands in the material of his shirt and wedged her leg between his thighs.

And his body had noticed. He was fully and painfully aroused. For a moment he allowed himself to lie still and watch her sleep. Her hands clenched and unclenched on his shirt, and he felt the imprint of each of her fingers on his chest. Her leg twitched between his, and he had to grab the grass next to him to keep from wrapping his arms around her. When she moaned once more, it was all he could do to keep himself from covering her mouth with his.

She was asleep, for God's sake! He told himself to move away, but he didn't move. His excuse was that he didn't want to wake her up.

He closed his eyes and tried to forget everything that had happened between them. He tried to imagine that he had just met Andi McGinnis, and that they had nothing standing between them, no bitter memories, no deaths.

He opened his eyes again, determined to move. Even if they had no past, they couldn't forget the present and their responsibilities.

Andi's eyes fluttered open, and she looked directly into his. For just a moment he saw pleasure and desire. Her mouth relaxed and her eyes heated to a brilliant blue. For just a moment she saw only him, and wanted him.

The need and desire he'd kept leashed burst forth from deep inside him, and everything faded except for Andi. He kissed her mouth, wrapping his arms around her and pulling her closer. Her lips clung to his, tasting and taking, and her eyes fluttered closed. She made a small sound in the back of her throat and struggled to free her hands so she could throw them around his neck.

He groaned once as he buried his face in her neck. When he raked his teeth over her ear, she shuddered against him. Then her hands snaked beneath his shirt and clung to his hot skin.

He drew in his breath sharply when she raked her nails over him. When she touched his nipples with a tentative finger, he felt a hot punch of need. He rose over her and shoved her shirt up to her neck, staring down at the plain white cotton bra she wore and the dark outline of her nipples beneath it.

His muscles trembled with the need to touch her, to taste her. Finally she opened her eyes and looked at him. When he saw the uncertainty in her gaze, the hesitation, he realized she was unsure of herself. The thought sent another punch of need through him.

Andi McGinnis was never unsure of anything.

He never imagined he would be able to put her off balance.

He reached out a hand and unsnapped the clasp of her bra. She gave an instinctive start, grabbing for her shirt, until he caught her gaze with his own.

"Don't," he said, his voice a harsh guttural sound in the silence. "I need to touch you."

As she held his gaze, her hand dropped back to the ground. He saw her swallow once, saw the brief flash of apprehension in her eyes. Then she grasped his shirt and pulled it slowly over his head.

His blood thrummed through his veins, shouting in triumph at her surrender. Her hesitation, her trembling hands, told him that she wasn't an experienced woman. He'd seen the brief telling moment of fear in her eyes. But she'd touched him, anyway. She wanted him. And he wanted her like he'd never wanted anyone in his life.

He ignored the need clawing at him, demanding release. Instead, he raised himself up on one elbow, then bent down and kissed her again. When he felt her relax, felt the softening of her muscles, he moved down and brushed the opened bra away from her breasts.

"You're beautiful, Andi," he whispered, touching one nipple, feeling himself get even harder as he watched it tighten. "More beautiful than I imagined, and I've imagined a lot."

She swallowed again and closed her eyes as he bent to take the nipple into his mouth. He felt her tense around him and he slid one hand beneath the waist of her pants. She was hot and wet, and she bucked against him when he touched her.

Slowly he teased her nipple with his tongue, then drew his finger along the dampness between her legs. Her head fell back, and she moaned. He touched her again—and felt her come apart in his hands.

He gathered her close and held her as the shudders racked her body. After a long time she pulled her head back so she could look at him.

"What was that all about, Chase?"

Her voice was low and still husky with passion, and hearing her say his name sent a curl of pleasure through him. He slid his hand down her back and pressed her closer.

"If you don't know, then maybe we ought to try it again. Clearly you've had a major gap in your education."

Hot color flooded her face. "That's not what I meant. I meant how did this happen?"

She looked bewildered and vulnerable and soft, and need for her coiled inside him, far too urgent to ignore. It made him feel exposed and vulnerable. Because his emotions were painfully raw and far too close to the surface, he gave her a lazy grin.

"I think it started when we kissed. Then I touched your breast, and you touched me. Then—"

She jerked away from him and sat up. "That's not what I meant. I meant, how could I forget what we're supposed to be doing? How could *you?*"

He wanted to tell her it was far too easy. He wanted to tell her it was so easy to forget everything but her that it frightened him to death. But he sat up, instead.

"Chalk it up to tension, McGinnis. It's a great tension reliever."

He saw her flush again. "You make it sound so crude," she muttered.

It hadn't been crude. It had been wonderful. He wouldn't soon forget how she'd looked and sounded. Her taste was a part of him now. He would dream about her every time he closed his eyes.

"It's no big deal," he said, praying his voice sounded casual. "But we should probably get going again."

She stared at him for a moment, and he could tell she wanted to say something. He held his breath, hoping she would just turn away and pick up her things. One bit of tenderness, one endearment, and he would be on his knees in front of her, begging her to touch him again.

But she didn't say a thing. She turned to pick up her pack and the still-sleeping baby, then turned back to him. There were flags of color in her cheeks, but she avoided meeting his eyes.

That was what he wanted, he told himself. He didn't want any complications on this trip. And making love with Andi McGinnis would definitely be a complication. It was far better that she think he was a jerk. It would prevent problems down the line.

"I'll paddle the canoe again," he said. "You can hold the kid."

"Fine." Her voice sounded stiff and cold, and he told himself that was exactly what he wanted. "Are we going to leave now?"

"We need to eat something first."

She looked as if she wanted to deny it, but he knew she must be hungry. He waited until she'd pulled a freeze-dried meal out of her pack, then he took one out of his own pack. It took only a few minutes to heat some water, and in another few minutes they were both eating.

After they'd finished and cleaned up, she hoisted her pack onto her shoulders and stood looking down at Paolo, who was still sleeping. She continued to avoid his gaze, and finally it hit him.

"Are you embarrassed by what happened between us?" he asked.

Color shot into her face again. "Why would I be embarrassed?"

He studied her for a moment. "I think you are," he said quietly. "I can see it in your face."

"I had no idea you were a mind reader," she snapped at him. "If I'm embarrassed, it's because what happened was so one-sided."

His heart crumbled as he looked at her. It was the last thing he'd expected her to say, the last thing he'd thought about. He stepped closer and put his arms around her before she could move away. Andi looked and felt innocent right now, and he was moved by her vulnerability. She fit perfectly against him, but he pushed the thought from his mind.

"It doesn't matter that it was one-sided. I loved what happened between us," he said into her hair. She tried to pull away, but he wouldn't let her. "I love knowing how much you want me. There's nothing to be ashamed of."

At that she reared back and glared at him, her eyes flashing. "I'm not ashamed of anything."

He bent down and kissed her once, his body tightening again when he felt her soften against him. Then he pushed his emotions into the box where he always kept them hidden and stepped away from her. "As long as we're clear on that. Now let's get going."

He made himself sound brisk and businesslike, and after a moment the naked bruised look faded from her eyes and she nodded at him. It only took a few mo-

ments to get the canoe back into the water. He helped
her into the boat, then handed her the sleeping Paolo.
Then, climbing in himself, he shoved the canoe away
from the shore and started paddling.

Andi watched Chase pull the paddle rhythmically
through the water and allowed her gaze to linger on
him. He couldn't see her staring, she told herself, so
she might as well get it out of her system.

Her body still hummed with arousal, and the memory of Chase's touch, his kisses, made her squirm
with need. Her face flamed again when she thought
about what had happened between them. He must
think she was a pitiful needy woman.

She wouldn't think about it, she told herself. It had
happened and she would have to ignore it. She had
too much at stake to allow herself to be distracted by
Chase Remington. It was just hormones and adrenaline.

But she knew, deep in her heart, that it was more
than that. She had always been physically attracted to
Chase, from the first time she'd met him. She could
chalk that up to hormones and chemistry and force
herself to ignore it. But now she knew what kind of
person he was. And that made him much more difficult to resist.

Chase appeared to be a cynical, bitter man, hardened by his experiences with the agency. And hardened by life, too, she suspected. But underneath the
surface, she was discovering, was an entirely different
man.

He was a good man, an honorable man. Chase

would deny it. He would tell her that she was looking at him through rose-colored glasses, that she was only seeing what she wanted to see. But she had discovered the truth in these past two days. Chase would not allow anything to happen to either her or Paolo. He would get them safely to Monterez or die trying.

And she'd seen him with Paolo. He was gentle and tender with the baby. Chase was a far different man than the person he presented to the world.

And that was a problem. She would have no trouble resisting the surface Chase. She would still be physically attracted to him, but that was as far as it would go. She would never begin to like him.

She actually liked Chase Remington.

Chase would be horrified if she told him. Her mouth curled into a smile and she almost laughed out loud. That was the one thing that was guaranteed to keep him at a distance.

Feeling much more cheerful, she rearranged Paolo on her lap and looked around. The sun was high overhead. They had only slept for a few hours, although it felt like a lifetime had passed since they'd lain down on the bank of the river.

"So what's our plan?" she asked Chase.

He glanced at her, and she saw the wariness in his eyes. She swallowed once, then met his gaze. If he thought she was going to brood about what had happened, he was wrong. She had to focus on their mission. Neither of them could afford to be distracted by this attraction that simmered between them.

Something in his eyes shifted, and she thought she

saw a reluctant respect behind his frown. "You're pretty single-minded, McGinnis," he said.

So they were back to McGinnis and Remington. Suppressing her disappointment, she told herself it was the way it had to be. "I didn't think we had a choice in the matter," she said coolly.

"You're right. We don't." He paddled for another few minutes, then let the canoe drift while he turned his attention to her. "I'm getting a bad feeling here," he said abruptly.

"About what? I thought we were doing pretty well. We haven't come across a soul all day."

"That's the problem." He set the paddle across his legs. "What were our choices for getting away from Chipultipe?"

She frowned, puzzled by his question. "I suppose we could have gone by car or taken this river or gone through the jungle on foot. Or we could have been picked up by a helicopter or small plane."

"Right. And El Diablo must know we didn't drive, because you can bet he's found my truck, which I hid in the bush outside of Chipultipe. You can also bet he's been keeping close track of any planes or choppers in the area, so he knows we weren't picked up."

"What are you getting at?"

He waved his hand at the dense curtain of trees and bushes that lined the riverbank. The buzzing of insects was a constant drone in the background. "That leaves the jungle or the river. You remember how tough it was to get through the jungle at the beginning of the trip? He knew how hard we would have to battle the insects and the heat and humidity. We would never have made it to Monterez if we'd tried to walk there. The river was the only logical way for us to go. But we haven't seen a soul. There hasn't been one airplane or helicopter searching for us over the river. El Diablo is too smart not to know this is where we would be.''

He stared out at the jungle gliding past the canoe. ''So why isn't he looking for us?''

A frisson of fear ran through her. ''Maybe he's waiting at the other end of the river.''

''Where? He has no way of knowing where we'll leave the river. We could pick anyplace between here and Monterez.''

''I don't know,'' she whispered. ''What do you think?''

''I think we're going to have to be real careful. And we're not going to run the river when it's dark. We're making good progress,'' he said gently. ''We still can reach Monterez in time to catch El Diablo. There's no reason we can't.''

''Assuming nothing else goes wrong.''

To her surprise, he grinned. ''We know something else is going to go wrong. It's one of the rules of every undercover job. Nothing ever goes smoothly or the way it was planned.''

''I'll keep that in mind for my next job,'' she answered tartly.

His grin faded. ''You do that.''

He began paddling again, pulling through the water

viciously. The canoe shot forward, cutting cleanly through the muddy water.

A couple of hours later, Andi heard the low rumble of thunder in the distance. She looked above her, puzzled. The sky was a bright cloudless blue. As she cocked her head to listen, Chase froze for a moment, then with a powerful sweep of the paddle turned the canoe toward the shore.

"Did you hear that thunder?" she asked Chase. "It's not supposed to rain. The rainy season isn't due for a month yet."

"That's not thunder," he said, his voice grim. "We're heading for a falls. And from the sound of it, it's a big one."

The water was moving faster now, and Chase's efforts to reach the riverbank were increasingly labored. The speed of the water was pulling them downstream.

"Put Paolo in his sling," Chase said. "Tie the sling to your body and make sure your hands are free."

Her hands shook as she slipped the sleeping baby into his sling, then tied the ends of the sling around her waist. Every second the thundering of the falls grew louder and the water swirled faster. Chase was making excruciatingly slow progress getting them to the shore.

"Okay," she yelled above the almost overpowering rumble of the falls. "Give me the other paddle."

Chase handed it to her. "Pull hard, Andi," he shouted.

She dug in and pulled with all her strength. After

a few minutes her shoulders burned and the muscles in her back cramped, but she didn't slow down. They were making progress. Ahead of her the water had begun to boil wildly, crashing around sharp boulders of black rock that rose out of the water like jagged teeth.

"Harder, Andi!" Chase shouted, and she reached down deep for more strength. Paolo was struggling against her chest, but she could barely hear his cries over the thunder of the falls. She didn't want to know how close they were to the edge.

A swirl of water spun the canoe around and almost snatched the paddle out of her hand. Then the canoe crashed into one of the rocks that rose from the river, and her head snapped back with the impact.

"Are you all right?" Chase cried.

She shook off the dizziness and ignored the pain. "I'm fine."

"We're almost there. Keep paddling."

She closed her eyes to block out the trees spinning sickeningly in front of her. Clenching her teeth, she concentrated on plunging her paddle into the water and pulling it back. The canoe spun again, and she heard Chase curse.

She opened her eyes and saw the edge of the falls, far too close. Chase was trying to reach a tree that hung out over the water. Gritting her teeth, she marshaled her strength and kept paddling. The canoe inched toward the tree. Ignoring the screaming pain in her arms and shoulders, she coordinated her strokes with Chase's and with each one the canoe moved slightly closer to the tree.

They were so close to the edge that the mist from the falls enveloped them. The water was a churning cauldron, water coming over one side of the canoe and threatening to swamp them. They were completely soaked, and Paolo was wailing in fear. The thunder of the falls was almost overwhelming now. It filled the universe, leaving no room for anything else. Her arms said they could pull no more, but Andi pulled harder. If they didn't make it to the riverbank, the thundering was the last sound they would hear.

Suddenly Chase reached out one arm and hooked it over the tree. The canoe jolted as the current tried to pull it toward the falls, but he held tight.

"Grab hold of the tree as soon as you can reach it, Andi. I'm going to try and pull us closer to the shore."

Slowly, inch by inch, the canoe edged closer to the riverbank. It was riding dangerously low in the water.

The edge of the tree was almost within Andi's reach. Judging the distance, she lunged for the tree, wrapping one arm around the trunk. It bent low to the water, but she held on grimly.

"Hold on," Chase yelled. She nodded once, concentrating on not losing her grip on the tree.

He wrapped his right arm around the trunk and let go with his left arm. He picked up each of their packs, and flung them toward the riverbank. They landed just at the edge of the water. She immediately felt the canoe float higher in the river. Chase had bought a few more moments of life for the canoe.

"We're going to try and move the canoe closer," he shouted to her. "Just do what I tell you."

The tip of the canoe was a mere couple of feet from the riverbank when she tried to move her hand again. She'd just closed her palm around the trunk when the canoe spun around and knocked her feet from under her. The canoe moved away, and she hung suspended by one arm from the tree, Paolo slung over her chest, her feet dangling over the roiling water below.

"Hang on, Andi!" Chase shouted.

She nodded and wrapped both hands around the tree, slippery with mist from the falls. When her hands started to slip, she hooked one arm over the tree trunk, then the other.

Her shoulders trembled with the strain. Then she looked down and saw Paolo, snug against her chest, his face red from screaming. If she let go, she wouldn't be the only one who died.

Her arms tightened at the same time as Chase's arm curled around her waist. "I've got you," he yelled. "Try and move toward me."

Nothing had ever felt as good as Chase's arm around her waist. She knew he wouldn't let her go— she trusted him completely. She edged a fraction closer to him, then moved again, ignoring the screaming pain of her muscles. Then both of Chase's arms came around her waist and he swung her and Paolo through the air. They collapsed in a heap on the riverbank.

For a moment she could do nothing but lie on the wet, slippery ground, holding the baby, her heart pounding and her breath wheezing in and out. Her arms and back burned, and the muscles in her legs trembled in reaction to her close escape.

Finally Chase rolled to a sitting position and eased her into his arms. "Are you all right?"

She nodded, not sure she had the strength to speak. Chase pushed her wet hair away from her face and examined her. His eyes were full of worry, and her heart stuttered in her chest. "I'm fine," she managed to croak.

"How about Paolo?" he asked.

She looked down at the crying baby. "I think he's okay, too."

"Let's take a look."

Chase eased the baby out of the sling and held him in his arms for a few moments. Then he looked up at her. "All his moving parts seem to be working."

"I think he's just wet and scared," she said. *Like me,* she wanted to add.

Chase shifted Paolo to his left arm and circled her shoulders with his right. "We never would have made it if it weren't for you."

"I'm the one who almost fell into the river," she objected. "You had to save all three of us."

"But we never would have made it close enough to the tree to grab on to it if you hadn't helped paddle. I wasn't strong enough to do it on my own."

"I think you would have been if you'd had to,"

she said. It was true. Chase would do whatever was necessary.

He shook his head and pulled her close. "It was a joint project. And it needed both of us."

She leaned into his warmth and strength and never wanted to move away. The falls roared, the mist continued to soak into them, all her muscles ached and burned, but she was content.

Chapter 8

Chase was apparently in no hurry to move, either, because his arm tightened around her. She thought she felt his lips moving over her hair, but she told herself she was mistaken. The only tenderness she'd ever seen in him had been directed toward Paolo.

Because her desire to continue to lean on Chase, to melt into him seemed too strong, she forced herself to sit up. His hand tightened on her, as if he wanted to pull her closer again, then he let her go.

"You saved the packs," she said, glancing at where they lay on the edge of the river. "I'm glad one of us was thinking."

"It was more a matter of lightening the load in the canoe," he said. "I was afraid we were going to be swamped before we could make it to land. I thought if I got rid of the packs, that would buy us more time.''

''At least we have food for us and Paolo.''

Chase looked down at the baby in his arms. ''Yeah. I could have *caught* food for us, but there isn't much formula lying around in the jungle.''

She looked at Chase, still holding Paolo, then at the falls that were so close. There was no sign of the canoe.

''I guess the canoe went over the falls.''

Chase looked toward the edge of the falls, where the world dropped away. ''It slipped away from me.'' Then he turned to her, and his mouth curled up in a grin. ''But it's no great loss. It had a hole in it, remember?''

She felt herself smiling back at him, giddy with the joy of being alive. ''Yeah, we couldn't have gotten much for it in a trade-in. In fact, good riddance. Right?''

''Right.'' He smiled back at her, and her heart stammered against her ribs. ''Now we won't have to worry about our feet getting wet.''

Her giddiness faded as she thought about their predicament. ''What are we going to do now?''

''I guess we start walking.''

She stared at the edge of the falls, thinking of how close they had come to being in the canoe when it went over the edge. ''We were really lucky.''

''That we were.'' He glanced at her, all the laughter gone from his face. ''No wonder El Diablo never came looking for us. He knows about these falls, knows they're not on the maps. Once he was sure we were heading down the river, all he had to do was sit back and wait. We'd go over the falls, and his problems would be over.''

"That came too close to being true.'' She shivered.

He touched her face lightly. "But we made it, Andi.''

Her throat swelled as she saw the tenderness in his face. "Yeah, we did.''

"Now we need to make it all the way to Monterez.''

"You're right. I guess we should get going.'' She struggled to make her muscles obey her.

"I didn't mean right now. We need to rest for a while,'' he said, shaking his head. "You're in no condition to begin hiking. And neither am I.''

"Okay.'' Chase was right. She wasn't sure she could stand up, let alone begin walking.

"Hand me that sling,'' he said, nodding at the soaking wet cloth she still wore tied around her. "I'm going to carry Paolo for a while.''

She picked at the knots, but her hands were still shaking too badly to untie them. Finally he pushed her hands gently away. "Let me do it.''

His heat surrounded her, and his scent seemed to overwhelm the smell of the jungle and the water. She closed her eyes and swayed against him, and he curled his arm around her. Everything she felt faded away. She was safe and with Chase, and that was all that mattered.

''Let's get away from this mist, then we can rest for a while.''

She'd been draped over him like a blanket. And it wasn't only because she was tired. Feeling her face heat, she stepped away and reached for her pack.

''Are you sure you can carry that?'' he asked.

''I'm fine,'' she said, her voice tinged with embarrassment. ''You can't carry everything.''

''Let's go, then.''

Chase stepped out of the reach of Andi's alluring warmth and pushed the first of the branches out of the way. Thank God she'd moved away, because he wasn't sure he'd have had the strength to do it. She'd needed him, and it was a powerful heady feeling. Andi didn't need too many people, he was sure.

The trees glistened with a fine coating of mist, and a spray of droplets flew from the bushes as they pushed their way through. He glanced over at her, worried. He'd seen her arms tremble as she lifted the pack to her back, and he'd seen her wince when the heavy straps cut into her shoulders. But he knew her well enough now that he didn't say a thing. Andi was fiercely proud of her independence.

Her hands trembled as they pushed branches away from her face, but she didn't ask him to slow down. She kept up with him, matching him stride for stride. He could only imagine what kind of effort it took. He knew how exhausted and weak she must be. His own arms and shoulders ached with a deep burning pain.

''Do you want to stop here?'' he asked gruffly. ''The mist doesn't seem as bad.''

Andi glanced at him, but didn't stop walking. "What are our alternatives?"

He hesitated. He didn't want to push Andi too hard, and he was sure she wouldn't tell him to stop. But he did want to get away from the top of the falls. Finally he said, "I'd like to hike down to the bottom of the falls. We'll be more protected. And I want to see what's down there.

"It's going to be a steep hike," he warned. "Are you sure you're up to it?"

She gave him a weary smile. "Are you kidding? That will be a walk in the park compared to what we just did."

As he peered into the undergrowth in front of them, he saw that the jungle dropped off sharply in front of them. "Up to it or not, here we go."

He glanced over at her sharply, and she looked steadily back at him. Was she simply too tired to argue with him? Or did she really trust him that much? When a flutter of warmth stirred inside him, he told himself that she was merely too tired to argue. It couldn't be anything more significant than that.

The mist from the falls made the ground slippery and treacherous. As the terrain sloped downward, Chase had to hold on to vines and bushes to keep from falling. He glanced down at Paolo as the baby jostled from side to side, but Paolo was quiet. His eyes were open, but he looked dazed. Chase guessed that he was tired and ready to fall asleep again.

He heard Andi grunt behind him, and he turned around to look. She had fallen and was struggling to stand up again, trying to get a grip on a mossy slick rock. Steadying himself with one hand on a sturdy vine, he extended the other hand to her.

"Grab on," he said.

She slipped her hand into his and pulled herself to her feet. She staggered once, then righted herself. It felt like she held on to his hand for a moment longer than necessary.

"Do you want to stop for a while?" he asked, trying to ignore the warmth that stole through him.

She shook her head. "Not on this slope. We need to get to the bottom." She rested her hand against the trunk of a tree and looked at Paolo with worried eyes. "How's he doing?"

"He seems fine. I think he's about ready to fall asleep again."

Her face softened. "I'm glad. I was afraid I'd hurt him somehow while I was hanging from the tree."

"He's a tough kid," Chase said, letting his hand linger on the baby's head. Then he scowled at himself. He had almost sounded proprietary about Paolo. As he turned to head down the slope again, he reminded himself that Paolo wasn't his kid. He probably had family in Monterez.

Jagged black boulders littered the slope as they made their way toward the bottom of the falls, the rocks oddly out of place here in the lushness of the rain forest. An idea stirred as he made his way around the rocks. He glanced at Andi, eager to ask her opinion, but he saw that she was fiercely concentrating on her effort to get down the slope.

"We're almost there," he said, wishing he could make this easier for her. She just nodded without looking at him.

Andi was as tough as they came, he admitted with another surge of respect and admiration. He couldn't imagine anyone else, man or woman, who would make the effort she had for the past few days and not complain. But she hadn't said a thing. And she consistently put Paolo's needs before her own. And his, too, if he was being honest with himself.

He skidded the last few steps to the bottom of the slope, then turned and caught Andi as she slid down the slick surface. He held her arms, watching her face. "We made it," he said quietly. "You did just great."

"It was no big deal," she said too quickly.

"It was a very big deal." His hands glided up her arms to her shoulders. "I know how tough that was for you, but you did it anyway." He pushed her hair off her face and let his fingers linger at the angle of her jaw. "I've never worked with a better agent, Andi."

Her face flushed pink and she glanced up at him. Immediately he wished she hadn't, because he saw the vulnerability in her face. Her eyes darkened as she stared at him, and her vulnerability changed to something primitive and more elemental. She wanted him.

His body tightened in response, hardening immediately. He wanted her with a fierceness and a passion that frightened him. He had never wanted anyone this way.

He drew her closer and saw the answering hunger in her eyes. Need hammered inside him, pounding in his head and his chest with a powerful elemental beat. As she stared at him, he saw the echo of his feelings in her face.

Suddenly he had to touch her, had to taste her. His body demanded it. She wanted him just as badly, he knew. Her eyes fluttered closed and her lips parted. He could hear the tiny moan from the back of her throat.

He bent his head and took her mouth with his, savoring her taste, drinking in her surrender. But when he tried to pull her against his body so he could feel every inch of her, something was in the way.

Andi's eyes flew open and she stared down at his chest. When she looked back up at him, there was appalled realization in her eyes. "I forgot all about Paolo," she whispered.

He looked down to realize that the baby was still in his sling, hanging from his chest. He'd forgotten him, too. He'd forgotten everything but Andi.

He started to take off the sling and set Paolo on the ground, but Andi had already moved away. "Where are we going from here?" she asked, her voice tight.

Chase closed his eyes, trying to regain control of his body. When he could look at her without needing to devour her, he opened them again. "We need to look at the map. But I had an idea while we were walking down here." He forced himself to concentrate on what he was doing. "Let's see if we can find the remains of the canoe."

"What for?" She stared at him, puzzled.

"It might buy us some time," he said. He held out his hand, and after a moment she took it.

He led her to the edge of the river, where they stared at the water crashing and splintering on the rocks, which waited at the base of the falls like hungry mouths. He felt a shiver run through her, and he was sure she was thinking the same thing he was. They had come too close to ending up on those rocks.

But they hadn't, and it was time to move on. "Do you see anything?"

"Not yet." Then her hand tightened in his. "Over there. Is that part of the canoe?"

A curved section of wood was trapped and tumbling in the water next to a large boulder. It was bobbing so violently in the water that it was hard to identify. "It could be. Hold Paolo for a moment, will you?"

He handed her the baby, then found a length of stick that reached the curved piece of wood. He shoved at it until it popped loose, then guided it to the bank in front of them.

It was half of their canoe. It had split down the middle, leaving jagged splinters of wood extending the length of the canoe. They stared at it for a moment, then Andi took his hand. "Thank you," she whispered. "Thank you for saving all of us."

He squeezed her hand, then let her go as he hauled

the canoe onto the land. "It was a joint project. You did as much as I did. And now we have more to do."

"Surely you don't think we can save that?" She gave him an incredulous look.

He grinned back at her. "I'm not a miracle worker, sweetheart. But I think we can use this canoe to help us make it to Monterez."

She shifted Paolo in her arms and tilted her head at him. "How, exactly?"

He squatted on the ground and turned the section of canoe over so that the edges of the seats were clearly visible. "We're going to draw a picture for El Diablo, one that will make our fate very clear to him." Chase swiveled around to face her. "I need a couple of Paolo's dirty diapers and an extra T-shirt of yours."

He saw comprehension fill her face, followed by admiration. "That's brilliant, Chase. We'll leave our things scattered on the shore next to the ruined canoe, and when El Diablo finds them, he'll assume we died going over the falls."

He nodded, trying to ignore the warmth that stole through him at her use of his name. "That's the idea. If he buys it, he won't keep looking for us. Maybe we can head directly into the city."

She flashed him a smile as she slung her backpack onto the ground. "What do you want me to leave?"

"Was there anything you wore often enough in Chipultipe that people would remember?"

She held up a T-shirt and grinned triumphantly. "This. It's my lucky Michigan State T-shirt. I wore it all the time and everybody asked about it. They wanted to know where Michigan State was.''

''Leave it spread out on the rocks there, near the canoe. And leave the logo up so they can see it clearly from the air.''

She spread the T-shirt, making it look as if it had been tossed onto the rocks by the violent water. For good measure she crumpled up a pair of shorts and wedged them between the rocks that lined the river's edge. Then Chase tossed one of his T-shirts onto the rocks and spread two diapers in the grass a little farther from the river.

''What do you think?'' he asked when he was finished.

She grinned at him. ''A work of art. It looks exactly like we were dashed to death on the rocks and our backpacks spilled.''

''El Diablo is going to have to come looking for us soon. He can't afford to wait too long.'' He surveyed their handiwork once more, then nodded. ''All we can do is hope it does the trick.''

''Should we start walking?''

''I thought you needed to rest for a while.''

Andi rolled her shoulders experimentally. ''I'm sore, but I'll survive. My legs don't feel quite so much like jelly anymore, and I'd like to get going. Why don't we take a look at the map and see what our options are?''

He got out the map and they pored over it together. She was close enough that he could smell her scent and feel her heat. He wanted to turn to her, to pull her close, but he forced himself to concentrate on the map.

Finally he put his finger on a place on the river. "This has to be after the falls," he said, pointing out a spot where the river made a sharp turn. "We haven't been past there yet."

"Then this might be the falls," Andi said, putting her finger on a spot not too far before the turn. "We went around a pretty gradual turn right before we hit the falls."

He peered at the map, then nodded. "You're probably right. So we need to head toward this road. Then we can take it into Monterez."

He tapped a red line on the map that was one of the main roads heading into the capital. Andi looked up at him, and he could see the fear in her face. "Are you sure that's safe?"

"No, I'm not sure," he said, his voice blunt. "But I don't think we have a choice. We have to take the chance and hope that El Diablo assumes we're dead. We'll head over to the road and see if we can hitch a ride on a truck. It's the only way we'll get to Monterez in time."

"All right." He heard the dread in her voice, but she stood up and reached for her backpack. "Let's get going."

He watched her for a moment and felt his heart move in his chest at her bravery. "All right, we'll get started, but we're not going too far. Just far enough to get away from the river. Then we're going to stop and eat something and rest for a few minutes."

She nodded, then glanced at Paolo. "Do you want me to carry him for a while?"

He curled his hand protectively around the baby, who was sleeping. "I've got him. No reason to disturb him."

She watched Paolo for a moment, a tender look on her face. "All right."

Chase looked at the map again, then got out his compass. "This way," he finally said.

They walked through the jungle, the heat and humidity pressing down on them like a physical weight. At least on the river they hadn't had to deal with the oppressiveness of the jungle itself. When they were far enough away from the river to be safe from the prying eyes of helicopters, he spotted a clearing and halted.

"We might as well stop here."

Andi slid her backpack from her shoulders. Her T-shirt was soaked with sweat. "I'd give anything to have that leaky canoe back."

"The ruins of that canoe are going to save our bacon," he reminded her. "But I don't think we'll have to walk much farther through this jungle. We should reach the road by the end of the day."

"Thank goodness," she said fervently.

They ate a meal and fed Paolo, but when Andi would have stood up to keep walking, Chase took her hand. "We need to relax for a while," he said. "Sit down."

Her hand shifted restlessly in his. "I'm fine to keep

walking,'' she insisted. ''Maybe we can get a ride into Monterez tonight.''

He pulled her close and wrapped an arm around her shoulder. ''We're not going to make the road at all if you collapse on the jungle floor from exhaustion,'' he said gently. ''And we're not going to get into Monterez tonight, no matter what. We can't take a chance on stopping a car or truck at night. We need to do that during the day, when we can see who we're stopping.''

''I guess that makes sense,'' she said after a minute. He could hear the reluctance in her voice. ''But I'm so afraid that we're not going to make it in time. I won't have Paloma's death be in vain!''

Her voice was so fierce, so determined, that he wanted to kiss her and tell her that everything would work out. But he wouldn't do that. He couldn't do that. If nothing else, he could be honest with Andi. He could give her that much, at least.

''We still have two and a half days,'' he said, closing his eyes and inhaling her scent. ''We'll get there, Andi. We don't have to take foolish chances to make it.''

''The sooner we get there, the sooner we can set everything up.'' Her voice vibrated with tension.

''But we're not going to get there tonight. So you might as well rest.'' He tugged her closer. ''Sleep for a little while, then we'll start walking again.''

Chapter 9

Andi awoke slowly, struggling to surface from the deep pool of sleep. For a moment she thought she was in her bed in Chipultipe, then she heard the jungle sounds around her and she remembered.

Quickly she sat up, only to become entangled in mosquito netting. Chase had covered her with it, she realized. Her heart warmed at his thoughtfulness as she peeled it away.

Chase himself was nowhere to be seen, and neither was Paolo. Stifling the fear that washed over her, she told herself that nothing had happened. Chase had merely taken Paolo with him wherever it was he'd gone.

They couldn't have gone far. They would both return in a moment. She sank back onto the ground to wait, then noticed her clothes. They were stiff and caked with mud from the water and the trip down the slope. She could change them while Chase was gone.

She had stripped down to her underwear when she heard a faint rustle in the undergrowth. She grabbed her gun and spun around just as Chase stepped into the clearing, carrying Paolo in his sling.

Chase stopped so suddenly that the baby bounced against him. His eyes devoured her, turning hot and dark, glittering green in the dim mottled light.

"If this is your way of saying 'Welcome back,' I like it."

His voice was low and harsh with need. Instead of embarrassment, Andi felt a hot flush of desire wash over her. She ached to move toward Chase, to touch him and taste him, to feel his hands on her. She swallowed once and watched his eyes follow the ripple of muscle in her throat.

"I thought I'd change out of my dirty clothes while you were gone."

"Go ahead," he said, never taking his gaze off her.

Blood thundered in her ears and heat rushed through her veins. If he was a gentleman, she told herself, he would turn around. And if she had any sense at all, she would do the same thing.

But she didn't move and neither did he. She wanted nothing more than to walk toward him, to touch him and taste him and let him see the need that thundered through her, but she couldn't do it. She had never surrendered control of herself that way. Even the few times she'd made love, she'd always felt in control.

And she wouldn't be in control with Chase. She wanted him too much. Need for him burned too intensely in her. The next time he touched her, the next time he kissed her, the fire in her would blaze out of control.

"Put your clothes on." Chase closed his eyes, but not before she saw the flare of dangerous passion in them. "Please, Andi."

She turned away quickly and fumbled in her backpack for clean clothes. As she pulled them on, she heard Chase behind her, setting Paolo on the ground. She tensed, wondering if he would touch her, but he moved farther away.

Her heart still thundered in her chest, and she felt like she was gasping for breath. "I'll get everything together to leave. Should I feed Paolo first?" she asked as she turned around again, fully clothed.

"I already fed him. He woke up while you were sleeping." Chase didn't look at her. "He's all set to roll."

"Thank you."

He scowled at her. "You don't have to thank me. You're not the only one responsible for him."

"I meant, thank you for not waking me up."

He scowled again. "You needed the sleep."

His mood had gotten ugly all of a sudden. "I feel much better now that I've slept. How far do you think we'll get tonight?"

"As far as we get. I have no idea what we'll find."

She bit back a sharp retort and sank down to the ground to wait while he boiled the water. Sniping at each other wasn't going to make the trip go any more quickly. It also wasn't going to defuse the tension that simmered between them.

"Sorry," he said gruffly after a few minutes. "You asked a reasonable question. I shouldn't have snapped at you."

"That's all right." She waited for him to look at her, but he was apparently too focused on the boiling water. "We're both tense."

At that he glanced up at her, and she could see the tightness in his face. Desire glittered again in his eyes. "You'd be smart not to forget that, Andi."

She swallowed while he held her gaze. "Don't worry, I won't."

"Good." He avoided looking at her while he poured the water back into the canteens, then re-packed the stove. "Let's get moving."

Their progress was painfully slow. There were no paths, no obvious trails through the thick undergrowth. They had to fight for every inch.

Chase stopped frequently to check his compass and adjust their direction. Andi would have just enough time to catch her breath before they would start pushing through the jungle again. Occasionally they would emerge into a small clearing, where huge trees towered over them. They always looked carefully for some sort of a path, but never found one. Finally, after they had been pushing through the undergrowth for what seemed like days, Paolo stirred in his sling on her chest and started to whimper.

"I'm going to need to feed him soon," she said to Chase. "I think we'll have to stop."

He nodded and peered over the bushes. "I see another small clearing ahead of us. We'll stop there."

In a few minutes they reached the clearing, this one slightly larger than the others had been. Andi immediately sat down onto the damp ground and pulled a bottle out of her pack for Paolo. As he sucked greedily, Chase spread out the map again.

"It looks like we're very close to a stream," he said without looking up. "We should be able to follow it to the road. It'll be easier walking."

"That sounds good." She watched Paolo finish the bottle, then stowed it back in her pack and lifted him to her shoulder to burp him. "Going through this undergrowth is slow."

At that Chase looked up at her, a smile softening his face. "I figured you'd think of it in terms of time saved rather than how much easier it would be to walk."

"We don't have all the time in the world," she said stiffly.

"I was just admiring your single-mindedness," he said, his eyes laughing now. "Don't get your shorts in a knot."

"My shorts are not in a knot." She glared at him.

He laughed out loud. "I know they're not. I watched you put them on, remember?"

Andi gathered up Paolo and slid him into the sling, trying to keep her mouth from twitching. At least the tension wasn't quite as thick between them. She slung her pack over her shoulders and followed Chase as he led the way through the dense foliage once again.

"There it is," Chase said a few minutes later. She stopped next to him and looked in the direction he was pointing. She could just see a glint of water through the trees and vines.

"Great." Her arms ached with the effort of protecting Paolo's head from the snappy branches. "I'm ready for some easier walking."

Chase gave her an amused glance. "You'd keep going twenty-four hours straight if you could, wouldn't you?"

She flashed him a grin. "I'd stop for ten minutes or so to eat."

"That's what I thought."

Chase pushed his way through the undergrowth and Andi followed. In a few minutes they stood on a small clump of tree roots above the stream. It was slow moving, curling through the jungle like a thin brown ribbon.

"Stay behind me," Chase ordered, peering up and down the stream. "And watch where you step."

He didn't move and Andi said, "Is something wrong?"

"I don't see any animal tracks," he said slowly. "I was wondering why."

Andi looked down at the stream. The roots dropped away to a smooth sandy shoreline. It looked as if it would be perfect for walking. "Maybe there's a better place to get water around the bend."

"Maybe." He turned around to look at her and Paolo. "Okay, let's give it a try."

He stepped down onto the sand carefully, then turned and offered her his hand. Her skin tingled when she touched him, but she ignored the feeling. They needed to concentrate on getting to Monterez.

The sand was surprisingly firm, and Chase let go of her hand. Then he turned and started walking, slowly. She followed, suddenly uneasy. Tension sizzled from him and she wondered why.

Chase took another step and stumbled forward. As she watched, horrified, he sank quickly to his waist in the sand.

"Don't move, Andi," he barked. "Quicksand."

"Take off your pack," she ordered, backing up carefully. She tried to contain her fear—it would just make it harder to rescue Chase. She took the sling off her chest and laid Paolo carefully on the ground. "And don't struggle."

He removed his pack, and she leaned over the quivering sand to grab it from him. He was still sinking, but more slowly now. She set his pack next to Paolo, then turned back to him. "Do you have any rope in your pack?"

"Yeah, but it's not strong enough to pull me out of this," he said. He breathed in deeply, inflating his chest, and he stopped sinking for a moment.

"I'll cut some vines, then." Andi threw her own pack off her shoulders and groped frantically for her knife. In a few moments she had cut several lengths of the vine that hung from the trees beside her. "Here, hold on to this."

"I'm not sinking any farther," he said, but he took hold of the vine she offered. "Go cut a good-size stick."

Andi scrambled up the embankment, glancing over her shoulder as she did so. She didn't want to leave him alone.

"Go, Andi. I'll be fine." His voice softened as he spoke, and she nodded.

"I'll be right back."

It took her only a minute to find a small sapling and saw through it. As she ran through the jungle back to Chase, she had visions of finding nothing but the smooth surface of the quicksand, its victim swallowed by its oozing depths.

"Chase?" she called.

"I'm fine, Andi. Just bring the stick."

He had sunk almost to his chest by the time she arrived with the stick. "Tie the vines together," he ordered as he took the stick. He braced it against solid ground and tried to lever his way to the surface. He rose a few inches, then stopped.

Her fingers fumbled as she tried to tie the ends of the stiff vines together. Finally she thought they would hold, and she tossed the end to Chase. He looped it under his arms and tied it in a knot.

"I'm going to try and lever myself out. You pull on the vines while I'm pushing with the stick."

Andi wrapped herself around another small sapling and waited for Chase to push on the stick. When he did, she pulled with all her strength. Muscles that were already sore screamed in protest, but she ignored them. Chase rose a few more inches from the quagmire.

"Good," he called. "Stop for a minute while I rest."

He leaned backward so that he was lying on top of the boggy sand. She saw his chest heaving as he struggled to get his breath. In a few moments he raised himself up again, then nodded to her. "Pull again."

Each time he pushed and she pulled, he inched farther out of the quicksand. Finally, after what seemed like an endless struggle, his shoes broke the surface and the quicksand released him with an obscene sucking sound. He lay flat on his back on the surface.

"Don't move. I'll pull you to the edge," she called. Slowly she tugged at the vines, her hands burning, until he reached solid ground. When he started to crawl out of the quicksand, she leaped down and pulled him to safety.

He lay on the ground, panting, covered with mud. Slowly he raised his head to look at her. "Thank you," he whispered.

She took his hand and cradled it to her chest. "You're welcome." She drank in the sight of him, remembering his hesitation before stepping onto the river's edge. "You were afraid there'd be quicksand, weren't you?"

"I didn't like the looks of that sand," he said. "It

was too smooth, too even. I was just going to stop and get a stick when I fell in.''

"I was pushing you to go too fast," she said, horrified. She gripped his hand more tightly. "I almost got you killed."

"Don't be melodramatic," he said, and he managed to smile. "Outside of Hollywood, very few people actually die in quicksand."

She would see Chase sinking slowly into the mud and sand in her nightmares for a long, long time. "Are you hurt at all?"

"I'm fine, sweetheart." He rolled to a sitting position and her heart turned over at his casual use of the endearment. "All I need is a bath." He loosened his fingers from hers and turned her palm over. "How about you?"

"I'm fine," she said, curling her hand into a fist and trying to pull away from him. "I wasn't the one chest deep in quicksand."

Instead of letting her hand go, he gently pried her fingers apart. He stared down at her palm for a long time, then he reached for her other hand. When he looked up at her, she saw the naked emotion in his eyes.

"My God, Andi. Look what you did to your hands!"

She eased her hands away from him. "It looks worse than it really is—kind of like the quicksand," she said brightly.

When she would have moved away, he took her

arm. "Your hands are bloody from pulling on the vines."

"Yeah, well, I thought about letting you sink, but I wasn't sure how to work your stove." She was uncomfortable with the look shining in his eyes.

His mouth curved into a smile, but he didn't take his eyes off her face. "Good thing for me I never taught you how to use it, right?"

"Right," she said. Her breath tangled in her throat as she stared back at him, caught in the unexpected tenderness in his eyes. She leaned forward, planning only on brushing his lips with her own, and suddenly he had his arms wrapped around her.

"God, Andi," he said, his mouth buried against her hair. "I've put you through one hellish experience after another on this trip."

"No, you haven't," she said, her voice fierce. "Paolo and I wouldn't have made it this far it without you. You saved us, Chase."

His mouth found hers in an urgent kiss. He tasted of desperation and need, and his hands trembled when he framed her face. She wound her arms around his neck, losing herself in him. He groaned and pulled her closer.

Suddenly he pulled away. "I'm covered with mud," he muttered.

When she opened her eyes she saw the need in his face, along with the doubt. "Gee, that's too bad. And here I'm wearing pearls and my best party dress." She gave him a smile. "It's a good thing we're right next to a stream, isn't it?"

A smile flitted over his face and he reached out and touched her cheek. "You're something else, Andi McGinnis. Did anyone ever tell you that?"

"Many times," she said dryly. "Usually it was you."

His eyes softened. "I didn't know you before. Now I do."

"You don't know me, Chase. Not really."

He put his finger over her mouth. "I know all I need to know."

Tell him, a voice inside her cried. *Tell him the real truth about you.* But before she could speak, he leaned forward and kissed her again. There was such tenderness in the kiss, such sweetness, that she melted inside. This wasn't the Chase Remington the world knew. This was the Chase Remington he kept carefully hidden.

It was also the Chase Remington she couldn't resist. Sighing against his mouth, she opened to him and wrapped her arms around him. When they tumbled back onto the ground, she twined her legs around him, pressing against him from ankle to chest. And when he rose above her, she opened her eyes and smiled at him.

"All that mud can't be comfortable for you," she murmured. "Maybe you should get out of those clothes."

His eyes darkened as he stared down at her. "Be sure this is what you want, Andi."

"I'm very sure."

"I'm not what you need. I have nothing to give you," he warned.

"I think you're exactly what I need," she said.

"I don't believe in happily ever after," he said, staring down at her as if waiting for her to challenge him.

She didn't want to think about happily ever after, either. She hadn't for the past twelve years. "Then let's just think about right now."

Still he hesitated. "What about the kid?"

She glanced over at the infant. "Paolo is sound asleep. If he wakes up, we'll be the first to know."

She watched his face tighten and passion flare in his eyes. "That's about as noble as I can be, Andi." He bent down and took her mouth again, consuming her with his kiss. She felt his passion and his need in the tension in his muscles and the trembling of his hands. And then she felt nothing but her own need for him.

It swept through her like fire, burning away all hesitation, all doubt. This was what she wanted. Chase had haunted her mind for the past three years, refusing to go away, no matter how much she'd willed him gone. He'd been a part of her dreams, a missing part of her life, ever since she'd met him.

She had been waiting for this moment, she realized. As he fitted her into the curve of his body, nothing felt more right. And suddenly she'd waited too long. She wanted to touch him, to see him in the mottled light that filtered through the trees next to the stream.

Her fingers trembled as she began to unbutton his

shirt. When she had trouble getting one button through its hole, he gently pushed her hands away. "Let me."

He pulled the shirt over his head and tossed it aside, then she reached out and touched his chest, running her fingers through the dark blond hair. Desire flared in his eyes, but he didn't move. He simply sat and watched as she explored him.

When her fingers tangled in the hair that trailed down over his hard abdomen and disappeared into the waistband of his pants, he took her hand and brought it to his mouth. "It's my turn," he whispered.

He pulled off her T-shirt. Without taking his eyes from her body, he unsnapped the front hook of her bra and let it fall away, exposing her breasts.

She had never sat naked while a man stared at her, and she instinctively moved to cover herself. He caught her hands and kissed them, then held them gently with one of his own hands while he touched her lightly with the other.

"It's a good thing I didn't know how beautiful you are," he said, his voice hoarse. "I wouldn't have been able to control myself this long."

She swallowed once, desire pounding through her, making her throb and ache for his touch. "Same here, Remington."

As he leaned forward to kiss her, his hands cupped her breasts. They swelled and ached, and he finally brushed his thumbs over her nipples. He swallowed her cry of surprise, then groaned as he eased her back onto the ground.

"You make me wild, Andi. You make me forget everything but you."

"Good," she said fiercely. She wanted him to be in the same mindless state as she was in. She could think of nothing but him, feel nothing but him.

Swiftly he stripped off his pants, then hers. When they both lay naked on the ground, he stared down at her for a long moment. Then his eyes darkened and he gathered her close.

His kisses were hot and possessive, reaching deep into her soul and branding her as his. He touched her everywhere, his hands stroking and caressing until she sobbed his name. "I need you, Chase. Now."

He kissed her one more time, then eased away. "Hold that thought," he whispered.

She opened her eyes in confusion to see him rummaging through his backpack. A few moments later he turned back to her, a small foil packet in his hand.

"I guess you meant it when you said you were prepared for anything," she murmured.

He gave her a quick smile. "But I'm sure glad I have them. I wouldn't want to put you at risk."

It was on the tip of her tongue to tell him that she didn't care, but she stopped in time, appalled at herself. Of course she cared if she got pregnant. A baby and a family weren't in her plans. What was wrong with her?

Then Chase kissed her again, and the uneasiness slid out of her mind. She pulled him close, and he slipped between her legs. She rose to meet him, joining with him almost fiercely. He groaned her name, and she wrapped her legs around him.

They moved together, joined completely, and he twined his hands with hers. Sensation coiled inside her, more and more tightly, until she exploded, gasping his name, holding him as closely as she could. He tensed above her. She felt him shudder, heard him cry out with his orgasm. Then he rolled over and cradled her on top of him.

Chase drew in a shuddering breath. He could feel Andi's heart beating wildly under his hand as she sprawled bonelessly on top of him. He wanted to lie on this riverbank forever, holding her close, listening to her breathe.

A warning signal flashed in his brain, but he ignored it. He and Andi both knew the score. He'd told her that he wasn't interested in happily ever after. She wasn't, either. They could enjoy each other while it lasted, then part amicably.

But his arms didn't want to let her go. He turned and nuzzled her hair, drinking in her scent. She pressed her mouth to his chest, and he felt himself stir again.

"Now you're just as muddy as I am," he said, draping a strand of her hair behind her ear.

"Hmm." She rubbed her leg along his, and desire flared. "I think I like it. It feels...kinky."

He grinned into her hair, remembering her surprised responses to their lovemaking. "Honey, you wouldn't know kinky if it stepped on your foot."

"Is that so?" She raised her head to shoot him a

look he was beginning to recognize, and he struggled to hold back the grin. He loved the way she snapped at the bait whenever he dangled it.

"I think it is." He stared at her, keeping his face straight but knowing she would see the laughter in his eyes.

"We'll just see about that."

She pushed herself up on her hands, and the smile faded from his eyes to be replaced by a look of fierce need. He wanted her again, more than he had just minutes ago. That had never happened before. Once he made love with a woman, he generally only wanted to get away. But not this time. Not with Andi.

He closed his arms around her and brought her close for a kiss. "Let's see how kinky you can get."

A long time later Chase rose above her and bent down to give her a kiss. "That wasn't bad, but I think we can do better."

She opened her eyes and gave him a sleepy satisfied smile. "We'll just have to practice, I guess."

He felt himself hardening again at the look in her eyes. "I'll hold you to that."

She struggled to sit up next to him. "You can hold me to anything you want."

He wanted her again, more desperately than before. They had just made love twice, pouring themselves into each other, and the need that surged through him made him uneasy. So instead of bending down and kissing her again, he picked her up and tossed her into the stream.

Sputtering and laughing, she smacked her hand against the surface of the water and splashed him. Then she closed her eyes and lay back, letting the slow-moving water run over her.

He definitely needed to get her out of this stream and back into her clothes, Chase thought as he watched her. Every movement she made was seductive, made more so by her utter unselfconsciousness. She was too innocent to realize what she was doing to him.

"We need to get rinsed off," he said gruffly, easing into the stream. "Paolo will be awake soon."

She shot up out of the water, a horrified look on her face. "I forgot all about him!" she cried.

"I hope so." He stood up, turning away from her. He was distinctly uncomfortable with his body's response to her. "I'm glad I had your complete attention."

"You know what I mean," she said, wading to the edge of the stream. "He could have been snatched away, and I wouldn't even have noticed."

His heart clenched at her words. Did she know what she was saying? He doubted it. Paolo had been the complete and fierce focus of her attention up until now. "He's right there where you left him," he said, turning around to pull on a clean pair of pants. "He's going to wake up hungry, too. He usually does."

"He's still sleeping," she said, glancing at the baby as she pulled on her clothes. "But you're right. He's been sleeping for a long time."

They had lingered by the edge of the stream for a

long time. Too long, he thought grimly. And Andi was going to realize that soon enough. "Let's get moving."

It took them only minutes to gather everything together and start downstream again. Chase turned his head as they walked around a bend in the stream to take one last look at the place they'd made love. It would be a part of his dreams forever, he knew.

"I'll never forget it, either." Andi's voice was barely above a whisper. He gazed down at her, feeling as though she'd reached into his chest and squeezed his heart. Her face was soft and dreamy, completely open. Her emotions shone out of her eyes, and he forced himself to look away. That look wasn't for him, Chase Remington. It was merely for the pleasure they'd shared by the stream.

But he couldn't stop himself from reaching down and kissing her lightly. "Keep looking like that and we'll never get away from here."

Her arms crept around him. "Maybe that wouldn't be such a bad thing."

For a moment he wanted to hold on to her, to let himself believe that nothing existed in the world except him and Andi. For a moment anything was possible. Then he looked down at Paolo, sleeping on her chest, and knew it wasn't true.

"Don't try to tempt me, woman," he said, kissing her again, then setting her away from him. "I run a tight ship here."

She grinned and slid her hand down his back, lingering on his rear end. "Parts of it are very tight."

"And other parts are going to be even tighter if you're not careful." He took her hand in his and kissed it, then curled her fingers into a fist. "Let's go, Andi. We need to get as far as the road tonight."

He felt like a complete jerk when the laughter faded from her eyes. And when they filled with grim reality, he felt even worse.

"You're right. I don't know what I was thinking."

"I do, because it's the same thing I'm thinking. Just hold the thought for another few hours."

A spark flared briefly in her eyes, then disappeared. "Let's head for the road, Chase."

They walked on in silence for another hour. The light was fading when he heard the first sound that wasn't part of the jungle.

"Stop," he said, holding an arm in front of Andi.

"What is it?" She turned to him, her face tense.

"Did you hear that?"

"What?"

"I think it was a truck, off in the distance. "Let's find a place to spend the night while it's still light. Then I'll go have a look at the road."

It didn't take long to find a small clearing twenty yards or so away from the stream. Tall trees surrounded it, with heavy undergrowth beginning just a few yards away from the trees. "This'll work," he said.

Andi nodded, and he saw the weariness in her eyes.

"Sit down," he said gently. "Rest for a while. I'll go take a look at the road."

He could see she wanted to go with him, wanted

to check it for herself. "Paolo needs you," he said gently. "Someone has to stay with him."

"You're right." He could hear the exhaustion in her voice and thanked God he could use Paolo to make her rest.

"I may be a while. I have no idea how much traffic this road carries."

She managed to smile at him. "We're not going anywhere."

As he turned to leave, he wished fiercely that her words were true. He wished that she and Paolo would always be there when he returned. The thought shocked him, then frightened him. He didn't want the responsibility of a family. He wouldn't know what to do with one. He wasn't family material. He was perfectly happy with things just the way they were.

But as he headed toward the road, leaving Andi and Paolo sitting in the jungle behind him, he realized that something had changed. In the past few days, both Andi and Paolo had become important to him. He would miss them when they left.

And they would leave. He knew that for a certainty. Because everyone in his life eventually left.

Chapter 10

Night had swallowed all the light in the jungle by the time Chase made his way back to the clearing where Andi waited with Paolo. She was nothing more than a dark shape huddled against a darker tree, but Chase's heart raced in his chest when he saw her.

"Andi?" he whispered.

"We're here." The shadow against the tree stirred, then stood. "Paolo's sound asleep."

"Poor kid," Chase said, glancing down at the baby, who was swathed in a white blanket. "He hasn't had an easy time of it."

"Thank goodness he's such a good-natured baby." The shape that was Andi moved closer, but hesitated before she reached him. He wondered if she was feeling awkward after what they had shared earlier. He reached out and pulled her against him, and she melted into him.

"I was getting worried about you," she murmured.

"There wasn't anything to worry about. I was bored as hell out there."

"What did you see?"

"Not a lot. There were enough cars and trucks that we shouldn't have any trouble finding a ride, and I didn't see any evidence that El Diablo is patrolling the road. No one suspicious came by."

"So we can head into Monterez tomorrow morning?" He heard the eagerness in her voice and felt a stab of pain. They needed to get to the city, but it also meant their journey was over. They had no reason to stay together. He reached into his pocket and fingered the leaves he'd woven into a small crude ring while he'd watched the road.

"Looks that way."

She leaned away from him. He could barely see her face in the dim moonlight. "There are parts of this trip I won't be happy to leave behind," she said in a low voice.

"Yeah, I know you love eating those freeze-dried meals cold." He wouldn't allow himself to dwell on what she might have meant.

Even in the darkness he could see her grin. "You know me too well," she said.

That was the problem. He knew her far too well. Andi's job would always come first for her. It had three years ago, and he had no reason to think that had changed. He took his hand out of his pocket and stepped away. "Let's get something to eat. Then we need to sleep."

She moved away as if he'd slapped her. "You're right. We need to think of the job."

"Isn't that what you were thinking of?"

Instead of the quick reply he expected, she turned away and sat on the ground. "I've been thinking too much about the job lately."

"What's that supposed to mean?" He squatted down next to her.

"It means that maybe I've been too focused on catching El Diablo. I've been directly responsible for getting two people killed. Maybe the price is too high."

"What are you talking about? What two people?"

Even in the darkness he could see her impatient look. "Come on, Chase. One of them was your partner. You can't tell me you've forgotten that."

"I haven't forgotten a thing. But you're wrong. You weren't responsible for Richard's death. That was my fault."

She shook her head. "That whole job was a fiasco. I should have left as soon as I realized you were interested in me." She looked away. "And that I was interested in you. But catching El Diablo was important to me, too important to do the right thing. So I stayed and Richard was killed. I don't think it was your fault. I'm not sure it was my fault. But it wouldn't have happened if I had asked to be reassigned."

"You don't know that's true, Andi," he said, and

he realized with a jolt that he believed it. "None of us has any way of knowing what would happen if we had chosen a different path. It's not your fault Richard died. Hell, it might not even be my fault. But we can't go back and change history. So it doesn't make sense to keep beating ourselves up for what happened in the past."

"You're still beating yourself up," she said softly.

"How so?"

"You quit the agency. I know how much you loved your job. And I know how good you were at it."

He stared into the darkness. "That wasn't entirely because of Richard's death," he finally said. "It had a lot more to do with Mac."

"What do you mean?"

"Mac sent you to spy on us. He didn't trust us, but neither Richard nor I had ever given him reason not to trust us. That was the worst betrayal of all."

"You're right," she said. "I was spying on you, and I've regretted it bitterly ever since."

He turned to face her then. "You were just doing your job, Andi. You have nothing to blame yourself for. I was upset at the time, but that was more about me than you. I was angry with myself because I couldn't keep my mind off you. Or my hands."

"I should have asked to be reassigned right away. You asked me to do that, but I refused. And I—"

He reached out an arm and pulled her close. "Don't, Andi. We can't change the past, and it doesn't make any sense to try. And it turned out okay in the long run. I love what I'm doing now. Hell, if

I hadn't loved it so much, I never would have taken this job. But I needed the money to expand the company. So here I am with you, again.''

"It's not just you and Richard," she said softly. "It's Paloma, too. She was getting information for me about El Diablo, and now she's dead."

"You can't blame yourself for that," he said immediately. "She came to you and offered her help. Informants know the risks they're taking. They know what can happen to them and they choose to do it, anyway. Paloma had been working for El Diablo before you came into the picture. She knew what kind of monster he is."

Her sigh rippled by his shoulder. "Thank you for saying that, Chase, but the truth is, I should have gotten her out of Chipultipe sooner. If I had, she might not have died."

"Did you tell her to stay when she wanted to leave?" he asked bluntly.

"No. She was the one who always wanted to do more. But I should have known."

"You can't know everything," he said. "You're not that powerful. I know you now, Andi. I didn't really know you the last time we worked together. You're not to blame."

She leaned her head against his shoulder. "I'm just beginning to wonder if it's worth it." Her voice was weary. "Too many lives have been lost. And Paolo and you are still in danger."

"You are, too," he reminded her.

"I don't count," she said. "I have to..."

"You have to what?"

Silence trembled between them for a moment. He felt her gather herself, felt her turn to him. Then Paolo whimpered behind them, and she scrambled to pick him up. Her relief at the interruption quivered in the air between them.

He wondered what she'd been about to say.

Andi searched for a bottle in her pack, then leaned back against the tree. "Poor Paolo. Now he has nothing but this backpack and what's in it." She shoved the pack with her foot, then froze.

"Chase, the backpack!" She turned to him, and he saw her eyes gleam in the moonlight.

"What?"

"When Paloma came to my house, when she was dying, she asked me to take care of Paolo. And she told me specifically to take this backpack—she told me where it was in her house—and put his things into it. She was very insistent. I was so upset at the time I didn't even think about it. But now I wonder why it had to be this particular pack."

He was already pulling it toward him. "Let's take a look at it."

He pulled out a small flashlight and trained it on the pack. It was a coarse material, obviously handmade. They could see nothing special about it.

"I'm going to empty it out." He looked over at her. "Was there anything in it when you filled it with Paolo's things?"

"It was completely empty."

Swiftly he took out the contents, then examined the

pack. Andi leaned over his shoulder, watching carefully.

"I can't take it apart," he said. "We still need it to carry Paolo's things. But we'll examine every inch of it when we get to Monterez."

Andi tugged it out of his hands and turned it over. "Take a look at the bottom. Every once in a while it feels like something's poking me in the back."

Chase kneaded the stiff material in his hands. "There's something hard here," he said, excitement building. "Let's take a look."

In a few moments he had carefully separated the lining of the pack and pulled out a computer disk. He held it up to show Andi. "I don't suppose Paloma had a computer, did she?"

"No." She stared at the disk. "She was lucky she had electricity."

"Then we can probably assume she got this from El Diablo's house. If this is what she was thinking about while she was dying, it's probably important."

They both stared at it for a moment, then he slipped it back into the lining of the pack. "It's safe there for the time being." He looked over at her and gave her a grin. "But I think your Paloma might have handed you El Diablo on a platter."

"We have to catch him first."

"We will, Andi." He pulled her close. "We'll get to Monterez tomorrow, then we'll have another day and a half to set everything up. We'll get him."

She set Paolo down on his blanket and carefully covered him again, then turned back to Chase. "No one else is going to die because of that monster," she said fiercely. "And especially not you or Paolo."

"Yes, ma'am," he said, drawing her into his arms again. "I'm suddenly very interested in staying alive." His mouth found hers in the darkness, and the jungle and all its sounds and smells faded into the background. Nothing existed but Chase. Her need for him pulsed just below her skin, flaring to life at his slightest touch.

"How do you manage to be so damn sexy?" he groaned as he nuzzled her neck. "I can't think of anything but you."

"It must be the darkness," she murmured. "It's hiding all the mud and dirt from the last few days."

He leaned back to look down into her face. "I'm not talking about the surface," he said. "I'm talking about what's down deep inside of you. I'm talking about Andi McGinnis, the sexiest woman I know."

A huge lump formed in her throat. But because she didn't want him to see how much his words affected her, she gave him what she hoped was a casual grin. "I guess you were telling the truth when you said you love your work. It's obvious that you don't get out much."

Even in the dim light she could see his eyes darken. "I haven't wanted to go out much. I couldn't get you out of my head."

Her smile faltered, then disappeared. Emotion gripped her heart. "I never forgot you, either, Chase," she whispered to him.

"Then why are we standing here talking?"

He took her mouth again, and this time she lost herself in his kiss. They moved together as if they'd been lovers forever, both knowing what the other needed. Chase spread his thin survival blanket on the ground, then eased her down to it. Desire raged to life, trying to sweep away everything else, and she felt Chase tremble with the effort for control. But still they moved slowly, tasting each other, exploring with trembling hands, touching everywhere.

When they finally moved together, Chase clasped her hands and murmured her name. She opened to him, laying her soul bare, giving him everything inside her. And when she flew to pieces in his arms, she could only say his name, over and over.

They lay together for a long time, holding each other. She was content to breathe in the fragrance of his skin, to listen to the beat of his heart as it slowed and steadied. Finally Chase moved away, and she murmured a protest.

He bent down to give her a lingering kiss. "I'm just getting the mosquito netting and some clothes, sweetheart. I'm not going anywhere."

He arranged the sleeping Paolo close to them and covered them all with the mosquito netting, then he pulled her into the curve of his body. "Go to sleep," he murmured.

"Stay with me," she murmured back, close to sleep already, twining her fingers with his.

She felt his mouth brush her hair. "I'm not going anywhere."

Andi held that thought to her heart as she drifted

off to sleep. And for the first time in a long time, she slept deeply and peacefully.

Chase awoke the next morning to the faint, faraway sound of a helicopter. Weak sunlight filtered through the trees—they'd slept longer than he'd intended. But that wasn't surprising, considering how little sleep they'd gotten the night before.

He listened to the helicopter for a while. The sound didn't get louder or fade away, and he smiled to himself. He'd bet money that it was checking out the debris on the riverbank at the bottom of the falls. Andi would be glad to know their ruse worked.

He glanced down at her, but he couldn't bear to wake her yet. They were twined together on the hard ground, her body pressed intimately into his. He wanted to close his eyes and forget where they were, forget what they had to do. He wanted to stay like this with Andi forever.

The hell he did. A cold fist of fear clutched at his heart. He wasn't getting attached to her, he told himself as he eased away. They were going through an extraordinary experience together. It was natural for the adrenaline to run high, the reactions to be exaggerated. Because that was all it was, adrenaline and nerves. Once they were safely in Monterez, they would both revert to their normal selves.

He wouldn't need Andi with this mind-numbing, soul-deep need that had filled him until all he could think of was her. It was nothing more than great sex, he told himself. That, and scratching an itch that had been bothering him for three years.

He slipped his hand into his pocket and fingered the small circlet of leaves. It was nothing more than a prop, he told himself. They would need to look like a married couple when they got to Monterez. The ring wasn't real. It was nothing more than camouflage to make them appear like a family—a family on the run.

But his heart contracted as he skimmed a finger along the surface once more, then carefully withdrew his hand from his pocket. It hadn't felt like a prop, or like camouflage, when he was making it yesterday. It had felt frighteningly real. And that scared him more than anything.

He didn't look at her again as he heated water on the stove. He'd smooth out once they were back in Monterez. They'd find Paolo's relatives, arrange to catch El Diablo when he met with the other drug lords, and that would be that. He would go back to his job in the States, and Andi would go back to *her* job.

This job, and the phony ring, would be nothing more than a memory.

He knew how important Andi's job was to her. She wasn't going to be willing to give it up. And there was no reason she should. She was damn good at what she did.

He scowled as he mixed the hot water with two packets of the freeze-dried food. "Time to wake up," he called to Andi in his most impersonal voice.

She stirred, then moved her hands as if she was

looking for him. His heart stumbled. "I'm over here," he said, his voice harsher than he'd intended.

Andi opened her eyes and looked at him. Her face softened and her eyes lit up. "Good morning."

"Good morning," he said gruffly. "Come on and eat. Breakfast is ready."

She gave him a smile that made his heart stumble again. "Is this room service?"

"This is as close as you're going to get for a while," he said.

She scrambled out from under the mosquito netting, then stopped. Faint pink color washed over her face. "Maybe I'll get dressed first."

She wore nothing but one of his shirts, and she clutched the gaping edges together in one hand. Turning away quickly, she fumbled in her backpack for clothes, then put them on with clumsy hands.

The fierce jolt of desire shocked him. He couldn't want her again. It was only hours since they'd made love. Instead of watching her dress, he turned away and concentrated on his breakfast. In a few moments she sat down beside him and reached for her own breakfast.

"So what's the plan for today?" she asked.

He glanced at her sharply. Surely she wasn't going to be so casual about what had happened between them the night before. Her head was bent over her food as if it was the most important thing in the world. But she still had the faint wash of color in her face.

He told himself it would have been better if she'd

been completely casual about making love with him, but deep inside, his heart rejoiced. It *had* meant something to her. But that didn't mean he was going to bring it up first. He was more than happy to talk about their plans for the day.

"You stay here and take care of Paolo when he wakes up. I'm going to check out the road again." He gave her a tight smile. "But I don't think we're going to have to worry about El Diablo looking for us along the road, at least for today."

"Why?" She sat up straighter and looked at him, her embarrassment forgotten.

"I heard a helicopter this morning. It was quite a distance away, but it sounded like it stayed in one area for a long time." She looked so hopeful he couldn't stop himself from reaching over and touching her face. "I'd guess it saw the stuff we left at the bottom of the falls and was checking it out. The pilot should be reporting our unfortunate demise to El Diablo right about now."

"Chase, that's wonderful!" She launched herself at him and threw her arms around his neck. "What a brilliant idea that was."

He found himself hugging her tightly, holding her against him and drinking in her happiness. "Yeah, sometimes I surprise myself."

"Not me. I've known all along how brilliant you are."

He pulled away from her before he could give in to the temptation to stay. "Then I'll take my brilliance to the road and have a look, just to be sure."

He hesitated, clearing his throat, feeling damned awkward.

"I made this yesterday afternoon while I was watching the road," he finally said, pulling the ring out of his pocket. "I figured we'd need to look married when we got to Monterez."

She went quiet and still. At last she asked, "What's that?"

"It's supposed to be a wedding ring, but it's not a big deal." He scowled. "Put it on," he said, reaching for her hand. He felt as if he was moving in slow motion, as if every second was an hour. As he slid the ring onto her finger, he said, "It's part of the show."

"I see," she said, and she bent her head to look at her finger. He couldn't see her eyes. "This is a good idea."

"Yeah, I'm just full of them."

He saw her lightly touch the braided leaves with one finger. It looked suspiciously like a caress. Then she looked up at him, her eyes carefully blank.

"What do you want me to do while I'm waiting for you?"

"Feed Paolo and have him ready to go."

"Will do." She gave him a wobbly smile, and he wanted to wrap his arms around her and tell her that he wished the ring was real.

Shocked and faintly scared, he turned abruptly and left the small clearing before he could make a total fool of himself. Thank God he had an excuse to leave, he thought. The tension must be getting to him. Either that, or he was losing his mind. Calling on his training, he forced himself to think about the next step of the trip. Getting into Monterez would either be a piece of cake—or a nightmare.

It turned out to be a piece of cake to get to Monterez. Three hours later Chase sat in the back of a truck with his arm around Andi. She held Paolo on her lap and gave him a weary grin. ''I guess after hiding in the chicken coop in Chipultipe, we were fated to end up with chickens on the last leg of the trip.''

Crates of chickens surrounded them, headed for the markets of Monterez. He could barely hear Andi over the squawks and screeches of the birds, and the smell was almost overpowering. Andi didn't seem to mind at all.

It hadn't been hard to find a ride. Chase knew that hitching a ride was a common method of transportation in San Marcos, and a truck had soon stopped for them. Chase had tied a bandanna around his blond hair, and they had spoken to the driver of the truck in the dialect of the region. The driver had shrugged when they said they had to get to Monterez to visit their family. He'd pointed them to the back of the truck and taken off again before they'd even sat down.

Now they were getting close to the capital city. Chase could tell both by the amount of time that had passed and the amount of traffic he could hear around them on the road. The crates of chickens blocked his view, but he knew it wouldn't be long before the truck stopped and they'd be in the city.

He bent his head to Andi's ear. "We don't want to let our driver get a good look at us when we leave. Try not to let him see your face."

He could feel her nod. "We must be getting close. Do you think El Diablo is going to have anyone looking for us?"

"I hope not, but I'm not willing to bet on it. With any luck he hasn't figured out yet that we're not dead." He took her hand, as much to reassure himself as her. "But just in case, we're going to disappear into the crowds as soon as we're out of this truck."

He leaned forward so he could see Paolo. "How's he doing?"

"He's almost ready for a bottle, I think."

"Why don't you feed him now? We don't want him crying when we're trying to blend in."

"Good idea." She flashed Chase a worried look as she pulled a bottle out of her backpack. "Have you thought about what we're going to do when we get to Monterez?"

"Yeah, I have. What about you?"

"I sure don't think we can go waltzing into the agency's offices," she said, giving him a weary smile.

"You're right. That's the last place we can go. El Diablo would be a fool if he wasn't watching the place, and he's anything but a fool."

"And we can't use your cell phone, I don't think." Andi shifted to face him. "It's too easy to eavesdrop."

"I thought we could get a room somewhere we can be anonymous. Then we can think about our choices."

"Do we have time to do that?" He felt her sudden tension.

"We can't risk doing anything else right now. We need a place to hide and think, and I want to get off the street as soon as possible."

"I guess you're right," she said after a moment, but he could hear the reluctance in her voice.

"Just because we didn't see any sign of El Diablo's men on the road doesn't mean he's forgotten about us," Chase said gently. "Our trick at the waterfall isn't going to fool him for long."

Before she could answer, the truck ground to a halt. They heard the sound of the door slamming shut, then the driver pulled off the crates to their right.

"This is as far as I can take you."

Chase scrambled off the truck, then helped Andi down. Andi kept her face hidden by bending over Paolo. It was a good move, he thought, watching her. Anyone who was watching would think she was merely being solicitous of her child.

He exchanged a few words of thanks with the driver, then turned away. Draping one arm over Andi's shoulders, he subtly steered her into a crowd of people. In moments they were out of the driver's sight.

Chase scanned the area quickly, but didn't recognize anything. As they walked down the street, pretending not to hurry, he felt the hairs on his neck rise.

He steered Andi around a corner, then turned again into a small alley. When she looked at him in surprise, he touched his finger to her lips.

''Shh. I think two men are following us.''

Chapter 11

Chase felt her quick fear and her quicker control. He spared a moment's uncomfortable thought at how easily he was able to read her, then put it out of his head. He couldn't afford to be distracted right now.

"Here, get into this entryway," he said, urging her into an open doorway. He slid in beside her, then waited for the footsteps he knew were coming.

They didn't have to wait long. He heard the low voices as the men turned the corner.

"Holy Maria, where did they go?" The first voice was full of surprise.

"They got to their destination, fool," muttered the second. "The next time you see some yokels from the country who are ripe for the plucking, don't wait so long to act."

"We couldn't do anything in the market square," the first voice whined.

"Then you must learn to be faster."

The voices faded away, but Chase didn't move. Beside him, Andi stirred. When Chase looked over, he saw that Paolo was awake. The baby was looking around with wide eyes, apparently fascinated by their surroundings. Chase couldn't stop himself from smiling at the baby. The kid sure had a lot to look at here in the city.

"I don't think he's hungry," Andi murmured. "I think he'll be all right."

"We shouldn't have to wait too much longer. Did you hear them?"

She nodded. "They sounded like nothing more than pickpockets."

"And not very bright ones if they thought they would get much from us." He glanced down at their clothes and felt some of his tension dissipate. "We're not exactly a walking advertisement for the good life."

He saw her grin. "No, we're not, are we?" Then the grin disappeared. "Are we going to be able to get a room, looking like this?"

"It won't be a problem where I'm planning to go. We need the kind of hotel where they don't ask questions and where no one remembers anything." He looked at Paolo again, who was patting Andi's face, and something squeezed his heart. "Let's go see what we can find."

An hour later they stood in a small room in a ramshackle hotel. "What do you think?" he asked her.

"Compared to where we've been sleeping lately, it's the lap of luxury," she said, setting Paolo on the bed and shrugging off her backpack. "Please tell me it has a bathroom."

"The clerk told me it would cost extra to get a room with its own bathroom." He paused, then grinned at her. "I told him my wife was in the family way and we would splurge."

As soon as he'd said the words, he wanted to snatch them back. It was one thing to say them to a desk clerk in a run-down hotel; that was their cover, and he would use whatever they had. It was another thing completely to say them to Andi.

She froze, then slowly turned to look at him. For a moment he saw the longing in her eyes, a need that made him suck in his breath. The next moment it was gone, and she gave him a bright smile. "That was clever."

It was too clever. He scowled to himself and turned away. He and Andi and Paolo weren't a family. And Andi wouldn't ever be expecting his child.

He was shocked at the disappointment that rippled through him. After the way he'd been brought up, he didn't know a thing about how families were supposed to be. A wife and children had never been one of his goals. And he was damn sure that a husband and children had never been part of Andi's plan. She'd told him herself that her job meant everything to her.

"I'm going out to take a look around," he said. He had to get out of this room, away from Andi, before he did something really stupid. "Don't let anyone in."

Her eyes flashed at him. "Do I look like a fool?"

She looked like everything he wanted. And he had to leave before he told her so. "You look like someone who can handle anything. I'll bring back something for us to eat."

He escaped from the room, closing the door softly behind him. But he stood in front of it a moment, reluctant to leave Andi and Paolo alone. It was only because they'd been together for the past three days, he told himself.

He heard a faint murmuring from the room. Andi was talking to Paolo. When he found himself straining to hear what she was saying, he shoved his hands into his pockets and walked down the dimly lit hall. The sooner they got this job over with, the sooner he could leave. And he intended to run as far and as fast as he could.

Andi listened to Chase's footsteps retreating down the hall. "He's gone," she said to Paolo, who wriggled with delight. "But he's coming back. And he said he'd bring food." She grinned at the baby and tickled his stomach. "We won't have to eat any more of those disgusting freeze-dried meals."

Paolo watched her with laughing eyes, his gaze following her wherever she went. After checking the room, she sat down on the bed and set him on her lap. "What are we going to do with you, big guy? Did your mother have any relatives in Monterez?"

Paolo stared up at her, his laughter chased away by the solemn tone of her voice. She gathered him close and hugged him tightly. "We'll think of something," she promised him. "Chase and I won't let you down."

She played with Paolo until his eyes drooped and he whimpered with weariness. She fed him the last bottle they'd made up, and he fell asleep immediately. Pulling out one of the drawers from the dresser, she made him a bed and set him on the floor. At least he wouldn't roll off the bed and hurt himself, she thought with satisfaction.

Then she headed into the bathroom. The shower was primitive, but it was the most beautiful thing she'd ever seen. She stood under the hot water, washing her hair and scrubbing off the jungle dirt for what seemed like hours. Finally, afraid that Paolo would wake up and she wouldn't hear him, she turned off the water and stepped out of the shower.

As she was toweling her hair dry, she heard the door to the hotel room squeak open. She reached for her gun, but realized that in her eagerness to take a shower she'd not brought it into the bathroom. Cursing her stupidity, she flattened herself against the bathroom wall and peered through the crack in the door.

"It's me, Andi."

Chase stepped into the room, and she threw the

towel around herself and hurried out of the bathroom. "What did you find?"

He glanced at her, letting his gaze run from her wet hair to her toes, and she felt desire stir inside her. When he looked back up at her face, his green eyes were hot with need. "What I found in here is all that matters," he said.

He moved toward her, but stopped before he reached her. "I'm filthy dirty," he said, shoving his hands into his pockets.

"That didn't stop either of us last night or yesterday," she said, clutching the towel to her chest as she watched him.

"Last night we were both filthy." He let his gaze travel down her towel-clad length again, then focused on her face. She saw him struggle with his control, watched as he pulled back. "Besides, I've brought food. Aren't you hungry?"

"Are you asking me to make a choice?" Andi couldn't believe the seductive words were coming from her mouth.

Desire flared in his face again, fast and urgent. "Maybe just postpone one of them," he said. He reached behind him and took some bags off the rickety table. "Food that's not freeze-dried."

"You drive a hard bargain, Remington," she said, reaching into her pack for clean clothes. "I'll remember that."

"You do that, McGinnis." He moved to the bed and sat down, but he didn't take his eyes off her. "Do you still have clean clothes?"

"Right here." Triumphantly she held up a T-shirt and a pair of shorts.

"Might as well get dressed, then." He leaned back on the bed and gave her a lazy grin.

She waited a moment for him to turn around, but when she saw the gleam in his eyes, realized he had no intention of turning his back. "A gentleman would allow me some privacy," she said, her voice prim.

"I never claimed to be a gentleman." His answer was prompt and his grin was lethal. "I'm looking forward to the show."

Two could play at this game, she thought. Although her first instinct was to turn around and show him nothing more than her back, she swallowed the uncertainty that filled her and gave him a slow come-hither smile. "Let's see what I can do for you, then."

The grin disappeared from his face, and he shot up on the bed. She saw the startled surprise in his eyes, and a fierce thrill of satisfaction shot through her. She'd managed to shock him, and the knowledge gave her the courage to continue.

She dropped the towel on the floor and slowly straightened. Swallowing once, hard, she worked to keep a sultry smile on her face as she reached for her clothes. She took her time getting dressed, keeping her eyes on Chase's. When she saw his taut face and hot eyes, she gave him a demure smile and smoothed her hands down the sides of her shorts.

"Now where's that food you mentioned?"

He simply stared at her for a moment, his tension

an aching presence in the room. Then he leaned back against the wall again and gave her a smile.

"It's right here. Come on over and get it." He held up a brown paper bag.

Andi sat down on the opposite side of the bed and reached over for the bag. "I think I'll just stay right here."

Chase gave her a grin. "Wise woman. I would have forgotten how dirty I was and how much I needed a shower."

Andi opened the bag to find burritos wrapped in wax paper. "These smell heavenly."

"I didn't want to go too far, and I wanted to stay in a place the locals would eat."

"What did you find?" Andi looked up at him in between bites.

"Not a thing," he said. "As far as I could tell, no one's looking for us. I didn't see anyone on the street who made alarm bells go off in my head. But that doesn't mean they're not out there."

Andi finished the first burrito and reached for another. "What do you think we should do?"

"One of us needs to get to the agency office." He sat up and pushed away the remains of his food. "We need to get them the information about the meeting and pick up a secure phone so we can talk to them without worrying about being overheard."

"I agree." Andi looked up at him, a challenge in her eyes. "I'll do that this afternoon."

Chase shook his head. "You can't, Andi." He held her gaze. "Think about it for a moment. El Diablo knows exactly what you look like. And he knows exactly where you'll be going. You'll be a target before you get within a hundred yards of the office.''

''And you don't think the same is true for you?'' she demanded.

''I'm sure he's traced the truck that I left in the village and figured out that it's connected somehow to your disappearance. But he's not going to have a recent picture of me. I've been very careful about that since I left the agency. Even my driver's-license picture is an old one. So I have a better chance of slipping into the building undetected.''

She wanted to argue, to tell him it was her case, that she would go to the office. But deep down, she knew he was right.

''And besides,'' he continued, ''someone has to take care of Paolo. You do that a lot better than I do.''

''You're wonderful with him,'' she said automatically. ''You take very good care of him.''

To her surprise a faint wash of color stained his cheeks. ''Yeah, well, he's a good kid. What's so tough about taking care of a baby? But he knows you better than he knows me, and we're in another strange place. He'd probably be more comfortable with you than with me.''

''You don't have to convince me,'' she said, glancing over at Paolo. ''The truth is, I'm not sure I want to be separated from him. And I wouldn't take him on a trip to the agency office. That would be too dangerous.'' She sighed. ''You're right, Chase. It would be best if you go to the office. It just doesn't feel right to stay here and let you do all the dangerous work.''

"You did plenty of dangerous things in the last few days," he said gently. "You deserve a little down-time."

"You did just as much as I did," she pointed out. "So that argument won't work."

"Yeah, but I'm meaner than you. So that means I get to go."

She flopped back against the wall, laughing. "I can't argue with that."

"I didn't think so." He stood up and headed toward the bathroom, shedding clothes as he walked. She was unable to tear her eyes away from the sight of his magnificent body. "I'm going to take a shower. I hope you saved me some hot water."

"There may be a trickle or two left."

He turned around and grinned at her. "If there isn't, you'll pay."

The door closed behind him, but Chase's face lingered in her mind. She rarely saw him so carefree, so relaxed. She glanced around the room. It certainly wasn't their surroundings. Andi didn't even want to think what kind of creatures the room held. Chase must be glad their little adventure was ending.

She should be glad, too, she told herself. She was close now, close to the goal she'd set for herself twelve years ago. She couldn't afford to let anything distract her.

But she already had. She glanced at the bathroom

door, behind which was the sound of water drumming against the tin shower stall. Chase had filled her mind for the past few days almost to the exclusion of everything else. And Paolo. She looked at him, peacefully sleeping in the drawer on the floor. Nothing would keep her from making sure that the baby was safe and cared for.

She leaned back against the wall and closed her eyes. What had happened to her? She'd lost her focus on revenge, and she had to get it back. She owed it to her parents, to whom she'd made a promise.

She was startled awake by the taste of Chase, filling her head. He was bent down over the bed, kissing her mouth. When she twined her arms around his neck, she felt his wet hair and his smooth face.

"You shaved," she said, her hand lingering on his cheek.

"I got a razor when I went out. I didn't want to give you terminal razor burn."

"I didn't mind," she murmured, reaching up to kiss him back. "I've never had razor burn before."

"What?" He pulled back to stare at her in disbelief. "How could you never have had razor burn?"

"The men I've dated have all been very proper and civilized," she said, rubbing her cheek against his. "They would never have taken me out without shaving first."

"It sounds like you've dated a bunch of wimps," he said bluntly.

Her smile faded. "I haven't dated much at all,"

she said, her voice quiet. "I never had time for dating."

"I'm glad you made time for me," he said, and his voice deepened.

She framed his face with her hands and stared into his eyes. "I don't think I had any choice about that," she confessed. "I've never forgotten about you." She felt herself slipping into deep water, and struggled to get to lighter ground. "And besides, I wouldn't exactly say we've dated, you and I. Unless you count our romp through the San Marcos jungle as a date."

His smile was lethal. "I always show my women a good time. I figured that was what would ring your chimes."

His women. Was that was she was? Just one of a crowd, a face quickly forgotten? She struggled to keep her voice light. "You were right, Remington. You knew exactly what would ring my chimes."

If this was all they would ever have, then by God it would be worth remembering, she thought. Without hesitation, without regret, she leaned forward and kissed him again. Her hands curled over his bare chest and tangled in the silky hair. He wore only a towel, tucked in loosely at the waist, and she reached out and pulled it away from him.

He groaned into her mouth and closed his arms around her. When he tumbled her to the bed and stretched out beside her, Andi's nerves hummed and her pulse beat wildly. She wasn't going to forget Chase, and she would make sure he didn't forget her, either.

But her determination to control their lovemaking was destroyed by Chase's tenderness. His hands floated down her body, caressing, stroking, drawing her heart into his hands. She felt herself trembling, felt herself turning to him and pressing close.

He held her gently, kissing her, murmuring her name, until she quivered on the edge of a huge abyss. And when he thrust inside her, clasping her hands at the same time, she felt herself tumble over the edge.

They moved together, their bodies completely in tune, his mouth covering hers. And when she trembled and climaxed again, he did so right along with her.

Andi held him close for a long time, awash in pleasure and floating on a sea of tenderness. "We even managed to make love on a bed this time," he murmured into her ear. "Don't ever say I don't treat you right."

"You know how to show a girl a good time, Remington, I'll say that for you." She kept her eyes closed and snuggled closer.

"And don't you forget it." He bent his head and kissed her again, a long lingering caress that was full of gentleness. "I need to go."

She tightened her hold on him for a moment, then let him go. "You're right." The light slanting in through the shutters was getting weaker. It was close to dusk, and the streets would be full of people heading home from work. "This is the best time to go. There'll be crowds to blend in with."

He propped himself up on one arm. "You're pretty

amazing, Andi,'' he said after a moment. "Most women would be whining at me to stay with them."

"Most women don't do the job we both do," she retorted. "I know what's at stake. Go."

He studied her for another moment, then rolled off the bed. She couldn't resist watching him while he dressed. "I have no idea how long I'll be."

"It doesn't matter. Paolo and I aren't going anywhere."

Chase looked down at the sleeping baby. "Do you want me to ask about him at the office? Have them get started looking for relatives?"

Her heart contracted at the thought of giving up Paolo. "I suppose you should. We need to know if Paloma had any family in Monterez."

"After Paloma volunteered her services, the agency would have checked on that. I'll find out."

"Be careful, Chase."

He was standing by the door, but he came over to the bed and dropped to a squat beside her. "I'm always careful," he said.

"Then be extra careful today. I don't want another death on my conscience."

Something flickered in his eyes, something that might have been disappointment. Then he nodded. "I'll be back as soon as I can."

She forced a smile. "Paolo and I will entertain ourselves. Just figuring out the stove so I can boil water will be a challenge." She frowned. "Can I use it in the room?"

"Open the window first. Then you'll be fine."

"All right." She stared at him, memorizing his face. Unable to stop herself, she reached out and laid her hand against his cheek. "I'll miss you," she whispered.

"I'll come back, Andi. I promise you."

"I'll be waiting."

Chapter 12

Chase lingered in the deep doorway of the shabby hotel, watching the street for a few minutes. No one even gave him a second look. When he was satisfied that there was no one watching for him, he stepped onto the street and began walking.

He took a roundabout route to the office, always checking behind him, always looking for the person who didn't belong. The streets were filled with people hurrying home from work, intent on their destination and not inclined to linger. Anyone pausing to look in a store window might be someone waiting for him; such a person would stand out.

As he got closer to the office, Chase moved more slowly within the crowds. When he was only a block away, he slipped into a café and ordered a cup of coffee. He sat with his back to the wall and watched the crowds on the street.

No one seemed to be watching the building that housed the office, and Chase frowned. He'd expected at least one person. El Diablo was too smart, too successful, to fail to cover his bases. The drug lord might think he and Andi were dead, but he would still have someone watching the office.

Chase leaned back in his chair and studied the building. He sat patiently, nursing a second cup of coffee, and was finally rewarded. A tiny flare of light flashed from one office, then disappeared. Someone had just lit a cigarette, he realized with grim satisfaction. And the only reason that person was sitting in the dark was that he wasn't supposed to be there.

With a surge of energy, Chase pushed the coffee cup to the side and threw some money on the table. Now that he knew where the watcher was, he could proceed.

The back of the office building faced an alley, dark and quiet. The sun had set and deep shadows filled the dimly lit alley. Perfect. Chase moved through the shadows slowly and silently, zeroing in on an open window on the first floor. In twenty minutes he was inside the building. He stepped into the agency's office and closed the door behind him.

An hour later he slipped out of the building the way he had entered. A sense of danger hummed inside him, and he waited in the shadows for a long time, watching the back of the building. After a half hour he'd seen no one, so he began to make his way back to the hotel.

Night had fully fallen, and he stayed in the alleys until he was several blocks away from the office building. When he ventured onto the street, he slipped from shadow to shadow, watching constantly.

No one followed him back to the hotel. He was sure of it. But just in case, he hung back and watched the entrance for another half hour. No one lingered on the street, no one passed the hotel more than once, no one showed undue interest in the shabby building. Finally he slipped into the hotel and hurried to their room.

Their room. His and Andi's. He was thinking of them as a team, as a unit, he thought uneasily. It was important to think that way about the job, but he was afraid it was spilling over into their personal life.

That would all end in two days, he told himself. El Diablo's meeting with the other drug lords was set for tomorrow night. After that, he and Andi would go their own ways.

That was what he wanted. He repeated it to himself again, more insistently. He wanted to go back to the States and pick up with his business. He didn't want any messy complications, any loose ends. He would say goodbye to Andi and walk away.

Life without her and Paolo would be dull and colorless. A spear of loneliness shot through him, but he ignored it. It would be best for all of them to end it cleanly.

He knocked on the door before he opened it and

stepped into the room. His heart contracted at the sight of Andi curled on the bed, a sleeping Paolo cuddled close to her. She had washed the baby's diapers and all their dirty clothes, then draped them over the furniture to dry. Bottles full of formula stood lined up on top of the rickety dresser. The room looked cozy and domestic, and a feeling of rightness settled in Chase's chest.

He shook off the feeling as he closed the door. He tried to close it quietly, but Andi shot up on the bed, groping on the table next to it for her gun.

"It's okay, Andi, it's me," he said as he dropped his backpack and hurried toward the bed. "It's okay."

Sleep cleared from her eyes as she turned to look at him. "Chase. You're back."

"In one piece, too," he said, sitting down on the bed next to her and taking the gun out of her hand.

To his surprise she threw her arms around him and held him tightly. "I was so worried," she confessed. "It seemed like it was taking far too long. Then I lay down with Paolo so he would go to sleep, and I guess I fell asleep, too."

She was pressed hard against him, and he closed his eyes as desire ripped through him, leaving a trail of burning need. His arms tightened around her, then he moved away. They had things to talk about.

"It took longer than I expected to get into the building," he said, standing up again. "There was someone watching the place, so I had to go in through the back. Then it took longer than I expected once I was inside.''

''What did they say?'' she asked eagerly. ''What are they going to set up?''

He walked over to the window and peered through the slats of the shutters. He didn't see anyone lingering outside the building, but he scanned one more time before moving away. The back of his neck itched, and he never ignored his gut instincts.

''I got a bad feeling at the agency,'' he said abruptly.

The eagerness faded from Andi's face, replaced by puzzlement. ''What do you mean?''

''The guy I talked to didn't seem too pleased with your information. He wanted to brush it aside.''

She bounced off the bed. ''Who was it?'' she demanded.

''Ed Olasik. I ran into him in the field a few times when I worked for the agency. He never impressed me as an agent.'' He gave her a thin smile. ''Maybe that's why he works in the office now.''

''I've worked with Ed before. He's nothing but a paper shuffler. He's probably just too lazy to do the work.''

He hoped that was all it was. ''Whatever the reason, he's reluctant to commit any men to an operation.''

''Why?'' Andi asked hotly.

''He was surprised as hell to find out what you'd been doing.'' Mac shoved his hands into his pockets, unable to shake the uneasy feeling that hung over him. "He said that Mac must have set this up himself, that he'd never heard of Paloma. And he said that because this went through Mac, instead of the office, they couldn't be sure your information is valid. He told me he was afraid that El Diablo had been deliberately feeding Paloma wrong information to pass on to you."

"Then why would he have killed her?" Andi paced the room, her face tight with anger. "How did Olasik explain that?"

Chase wanted to reach out and punch a hole in the wall. His frustration, suspicion and anger trembled, held in check by a fine thread. Then he shoved his hands into his pockets. "El Diablo was cleaning up his own mess. 'Just tidying up' is the expression Olasik used."

"He's wrong," she said hotly. "You've got to make them see that."

"I tried, Andi," he said wearily. "I tried for over an hour. The best I could get out of him is that he would consider sending some men if I could find another source who would confirm the meeting."

"What's *wrong* with Olasik?" She paced the room, her face rigid with anger. "We risked our lives to get the agency this information. How can he just ignore it?"

"He's afraid of a trap," he said. "He's afraid he'll be held responsible if things go wrong. Or worse, he'll end up looking like a fool."

"He's going to look worse than a fool if El Diablo gets this cartel up and running," she said viciously.

"When cocaine and other drugs start flooding the U.S., Olasik is going to have a lot of explaining to do."

"The guy is a bureaucrat, Andi," he said, putting his hands on her arms. He ached to do more, to draw her into his arms, but he knew he had to keep a level head. "They're always trying to cover their own behinds."

"Then what are we going to do?" The words were a cry of despair. He pulled her close, unable to resist. She vibrated with tension. "How can we change his mind?"

"Three ways." Reluctantly he let her go and stepped back. He needed a clear head. "First, I got him to give me a cell phone that's been fitted with a scrambler. Now we can make calls without having to worry about being intercepted."

"Who are we going to call?"

He gave her a grim smile. "We're going to start with Mac. This operation started and ended with Mac. He'll have the authority to get something done."

Andi froze. "You're going to call Mac? I thought the two of you no longer had any contact."

"I haven't spoken to him in three years. I guess it's been long enough."

Andi's face softened as she watched him. "You're willing to talk to Mac because of me?" she whispered.

"Hell, Andi, I'm not working for him anymore. How long can one person hold a grudge?"

"You feel he betrayed you," she said.

"I'll get over it. This is more important."

"I can call him, if you like. Then you won't have to talk to him."

He sighed. "Thank you, Andi. I'm sure he'd listen to you, too, but this is something I have to do. I've let this go on long enough. I realized as I was walking back here that I had a choice between my pride and catching El Diablo. And believe me, that put things into perspective. I'll talk to Mac and make sure he pulls enough strings to get an operation going out at that abandoned airstrip tomorrow night."

"Thank you, Chase."

She glowed at him, her eyes soft with understanding. His heart moved at the sight of her, and because that scared him, he said gruffly, "It's no big deal. It's just part of the job."

"It is a big deal," she insisted. "It means a lot to me."

"I'm glad I can make someone happy," he said, retreating behind humor to hide the fear that ate at him as she watched him. "I sure didn't make Olasik at the agency office very happy."

She watched him for a moment, then said, "What are the other two things we're going to do?"

"I'm going to try and find some of my old contacts. They might know something about this meeting. If I can bring in more than one source, the agency's more likely to act on it."

The warm look in her eyes was leached away, replaced by fear. "That sounds dangerous," she said quietly.

He shrugged. "It's something I used to do all the time." He shot her a look. "You do, too. So what's the big deal?"

"The big deal is that you haven't worked in this area for three years. How will you know where to find people? It's too dangerous to go wandering around the streets of Monterez. El Diablo is no doubt still looking for us."

"He sure as hell has someone watching the agency office building. But we still don't know if he's figured out our little game. It might be perfectly safe on the street." He gave her a grim smile. "And as for finding my informants, people are creatures of habit. I'm betting they still hang out in the same bars and low-life dives they did before."

"Maybe they've changed loyalties," she said, biting her lower lip. "How will you know they're not working for El Diablo now?"

"You're going to have to trust me, Andi. I'm pretty good at reading people. If the information is out there, I'll get it."

"I do trust you, Chase. You know that. I'm just worried about you."

"I thought you were worried about catching El Diablo."

"I am, but you're more important than that. I don't want you to get hurt."

He softened at the look on her face. Clearly she was frightened for him. "I'm not going to get hurt. I've survived a lot worse than the streets of Monterez."

He couldn't resist pulling her close again, and she nestled into him as if she belonged there. He closed his eyes, wishing he could stand like this forever, wishing they didn't have to deal with the real world. When he bent his head to kiss her, she clung to him as if she wished the same thing.

Finally he forced himself to step away. "You can't come with me," he said, recognizing the look on her face and anticipating her next request. "These bars aren't family establishments. Women and children don't go near them. It would only endanger you and Paolo and scare away my informants."

She gave him a tiny smile. "It was just a thought. You know me too well, I guess."

He did know her too well. That sense of connection he'd felt at the beginning of the trip had only gotten stronger. Now it seemed he could read her mind, and she could read his. The thought made him uneasy again, and he decided to change the subject.

"Speaking of Paolo, I found a file on Paloma when Olasik was out of the room. He'd never seen it because he didn't know to look."

"What did you find?"

"Apparently Paloma didn't have any family at all. That's unusual enough in this country that the bureaucrats checked her out pretty carefully. They were afraid she was hiding something, and they didn't want unknown relatives cropping up and screaming bloody murder at them if something happened to Paloma."

"There isn't anyone?" Andi glanced at the baby, sleeping on the bed.

He followed her gaze. "Not a soul. Both she and her husband were only children, and both sets of parents are dead. So there isn't anyone for Paolo."

"Poor baby," she murmured.

"Olasik called up an orphanage in Monterez. We have an appointment there tomorrow morning."

"An orphanage?" She turned horrified eyes on him.

He held up his hands. "It wasn't my idea. But what alternatives do we have?"

"I don't want to put him in an orphanage," she whispered.

She looked devastated. He put an arm around her shoulders and squeezed. "We have to go take a look," he said gently. "He has no place else to go. That's where children like Paolo are raised in San Marco."

"Who would hold him when he cried?" she said, staring at the baby. "Who would know what kinds of games he likes to play?"

"Andi, we're just looking at the place. I didn't say we were going to leave him there. Maybe it'll turn out to be wonderful."

"An orphanage? Wonderful?"

"Don't worry about it tonight," he said, squeezing her shoulders again, then moving away before he was tempted to stay. He had things he had to do tonight. "Why don't you go back to sleep? I'm going to head out. It's a little early, but that'll give me a chance to look around."

"Please be careful, Chase." She turned around to

look at him and he saw the fear in her eyes. It made him want to wrap his arms around her again.

"Don't worry, Andi. I won't take any stupid chances."

She gave him a tiny smile. "I should probably ask you to define stupid, but I don't think I want to know."

He reached into his backpack and pulled out the cell phone the agency had given him. "Keep this so I can call you if I need to." He reached in again and pulled out a laptop computer. "They gave me this, too. I thought we could take a look at that disk and see what's on it."

"That's going to be method number three to twist Olasik's arm, I assume?"

"We can hope. We have no idea what's on the disk, but maybe we can use it. We'll take a look later."

Andi glanced down at the phone and the computer, both sleek pieces of technology that looked completely out of place in the shabby hotel room. "I don't want to sound like a broken record, but El Diablo has already claimed too many victims. Please be careful, Chase."

"That's my middle name."

"I thought your middle name was 'take a chance,'" she said somberly.

"Not tonight." They had too much unfinished business between them. The thought came from nowhere, and he tried to push it away, but it wouldn't leave.

He and Andi had to finish this job. That was all he meant, he told himself. Their personal relationship would be over when the job was over. That was what he wanted.

Wasn't it?

The answer eluded him, and he didn't like the uncertainty. So he pulled Andi close and kissed her, then moved away before he could kiss her again. All he really wanted to do was lie down in the bed with her and stay there for a couple of years.

But he had a job to do. "Lock the door behind me," he said and left.

Andi watched him go, her arms aching to hold him again, her heart breaking. *Please, God,* she prayed, *send him back to us.*

She and Paolo needed him. She looked at the bed, where the baby was still sleeping. She had a feeling Chase needed them, too.

It was almost dawn when the sound of footsteps in the hallway outside the room jerked her attention away from the computer. Andi looked up from the screen, her fingers poised over the keyboard, and felt her heart leap.

As soon as she heard the key in the lock she jumped off the bed and hurried to the door. Chase stepped in and she threw her arms around his neck. "Are you all right?"

He leaned his forehead against hers. "Other than being exhausted and stinking of cigarettes and whiskey, yes." He tightened his arms around her. "But I guess the hardships were worth it. I like being greeted this way.''

"I missed you.'' Andi pressed a kiss to his mouth, then stepped back. "Did you get any information?''

He brushed a lock of hair out of her face and nodded. She could see the lines of weariness on his face. "I talked to three guys. The meeting is still on, but the location has been moved. Some other abandoned airstrip.'' His mouth settled into a grim line. "Apparently El Diablo discovered our little charade with the broken canoe and the clothes strewn on the rocks. I was surprised he hadn't canceled the meeting altogether, but apparently he hasn't.''

"He can't,'' she said, nodding at the computer on the bed. "I'll show you in a minute. Did you find out where the meeting's going to be?''

"Yeah, but it cost me the rest of my money. The guy was scared to give me the information. He wanted to leave Monterez and go far far away. El Diablo has a long reach in this country.''

"That doesn't matter. We can get more money,'' she said impatiently. "My salary for the past three months is sitting in the bank.''

He watched her with a peculiar light in his eyes. "So money isn't what drew you to this job.''

"Not at all.'' Her answer was prompt.

Before she could ask him another question, he said, "Sometime we're going to have to talk about what does motivate you to do this job.''

"Now isn't the time to get into life stories,'' she

said, too quickly. "Did you call Olasik at the agency office with this information?"

He hesitated, then shook his head. "I'm going to call Mac. I'd rather have him coordinate this operation." He took a deep breath, as if he was jumping into water over his head, then said, "Something about Olasik bothered me last night, Andi. He's probably just a lazy bureaucrat, but he raised the hairs on the back of my neck. I'm not going to tell him about the location being changed. And I'm going to suggest that Mac not tell him, either."

Chase had just trusted her with an instinct, with a feeling that was almost too vague to be qualified. He trusted her enough to tell her exactly what he was doing. She gave him a smile around the huge lump in the back of her throat. "I always follow my gut instincts," she said. "Sometimes that's all you have."

Relief filled his face. "I was hoping you'd agree with me."

"Absolutely." She remembered the computer. "Come see what I found."

For the first time he glanced at the bed, where she'd sat with the computer. "Did you take a look at the disk?"

"Yes, I did." She gave him a satisfied grin. "And I know why El Diablo couldn't afford to postpone this meeting."

"Show me."

He sat down beside her on the bed, staring at the computer screen. "It took a long time to decode the information," she began. "When I first opened the disk, it was a meaningless jumble of numbers and letters. But when I broke his code, I hit the jackpot."

She leaned forward and began pushing buttons. A long list of names and addresses scrolled down the screen. "I think these are his contacts in the States," she said. "All the distributors who sell his drugs for him."

"How did you come to that conclusion?" Chase asked, still staring at the screen.

"See these letters next to the names? I think those are his code for what drugs he sells each person. Once I got the disk decoded, it was simple—*c* for cocaine, *h* for heroin, *m* for marijuana. Now look at this next list."

She scrolled down. "I think these are his people who are also dealing with his two rivals in South America. There are an awful lot of names on this list." She sat back and gave a triumphant smile. "My suspicion is that these two in South America joined together to try and muscle El Diablo out of business. He either fights back or merges with them. No one has ever said that El Diablo is stupid. I'm sure he saw the benefits of merging over fighting. And with the three of them combined, all of them will be a lot more powerful."

"So you think he's in a rush to get this merger going so he isn't forced out of the market?"

She nodded. "Yes. I could be way off base, but the data seems to support that. And it would certainly explain why he would take such a risk and meet with the other two drug lords. He hardly ever comes out of his compound anymore.''

"You could be right,'' Chase said slowly. He scrolled down the list of names again, studying it carefully. "And even if you're wrong, this computer disk is worth its weight in gold. Do you know how much damage we'll be able to do to his network with this information?''

"We should be able to shut him down. But it won't count unless El Diablo himself is behind bars.''

She heard the passionate rise in her voice and wished that she'd been more careful. Chase glanced over at her, speculation in his eyes, but he didn't say a thing. After a few more minutes he turned off the computer and set it on the table by the bed.

"I'm beat,'' he said, stripping off his clothes. "We can continue this discussion a little later in the morning, but right now, I have to sleep.''

She wondered what discussion that would be, but didn't want to ask. Instead, she nodded. Checking on Paolo, who was sleeping soundly in his dresser drawer on the floor, she climbed into bed beside Chase. Suddenly she, too, was overwhelmed by the need for sleep.

He pulled her close and nuzzled his face into her neck. He kissed her once, then was asleep. She heard his steady even breathing.

She was where she belonged, she thought drowsily. Relaxing her body into his, she fell into a deep dreamless sleep.

* * *

Andi awoke groggy and disoriented. She thought she'd heard Paolo crying, but when she looked over, she saw he was still asleep in the drawer. Then she heard the noise again, and she realized that another baby was crying. A baby somewhere outside the hotel.

She sat up. Chase was asleep, sprawled beside her in the bed. His dark-blond chest hairs glinted in the sunlight that filtered through the shutters, and his face looked relaxed. Once again she noticed the laugh lines around his eyes and wondered if she would ever see him laughing on a regular basis.

It was better not to think about that, she told herself. Chase had made it plain he wasn't interested in a long-term relationship, and she wasn't, either. Or at least she hadn't been before this trip.

As she sat staring at Chase, regretting what couldn't be, he stirred. Without opening his eyes he reached for her. When he curled his arm around her, she lay back down.

"I forgot something last night before I fell asleep," he said, his voice low and gravelly.

"What was that?" She forced herself to concentrate on the case, on El Diablo, while her body responded to Chase's touch.

"This." He raised himself on one elbow and covered her mouth with his, and her bones turned to water. Everything but Chase vanished from her mind.

They joined together as if they'd been lovers for years, each knowing what the other needed. Chase kissed her mouth, her neck, her breasts, every touch driving her higher and higher. When she pulled him closer, luxuriating in the hardness of his muscles and the heat of his skin, he groaned into her neck. And when they clasped hands and flew off the peak together, she cried out his name.

They were both breathing heavily as they lay on the bed, their arms and legs tangled together. Finally Chase sighed and rolled over, carrying her with him so that she was staring down at him.

"Good morning, Andi," he said, his mouth curling into an intimate smile.

"That was certainly a good way to start the morning," she answered, snuggling closer to him.

He trailed his hand down her back, lingering on her hip. "Mmm," he agreed.

She wanted to curl into him and stay forever, drinking in his musky male smell. Then Paolo let out a yell, and she bolted upright.

"Back to reality," he said, easing her away from him.

Chapter 13

Chase watched Andi scramble off the bed and take Paolo out of his makeshift bed. He stopped screaming immediately and smiled as Andi murmured to him.

She picked up a bottle off the dresser, then climbed back into bed. Leaning back against the wall, she offered the bottle to Paolo, then smiled down at him as he ate.

Andi was tousled and flushed from their lovemaking, and Paolo was waving his chubby arms and legs in the air as he sucked the nipple. Chase leaned back against the wall and watched them, unable to tear his gaze away.

Andi looked up and gave him an intimate smile, and he reached out and touched her face. She seemed to glow for a moment, then looked back down at Paolo. Chase watched them for a few seconds longer, basking in the sight, before realizing what he was doing. He'd been imagining that he and Andi and Paolo were a family, and that this cozy little domestic scene would be repeated every day.

With a spurt of fear he launched himself off the bed and muttered, "I'll get a shower while you finish with him."

"All right."

He heard the question in her voice, but he couldn't look at her. He was afraid she'd see the fear in his face.

When he emerged from the tiny bathroom fifteen minutes later, Paolo was lying on a blanket on the floor and Andi had thrown on some of the clothes she'd washed the day before. She gave him a bright smile.

"What do we do first this morning?"

He wanted to recapture the intimacy they'd shared just minutes ago, but he knew that wouldn't be smart. So he picked up the phone. "I'm going to call Mac."

"Fine. I'll take a shower while you're doing that."

He watched the door close behind her, thinking it was typical of Andi. She was considerate enough to give him space to make the call privately. She knew it was going to be difficult for him. Another woman would have stayed in the room, eager to hear all the details. But Andi just gave him a smile and disappeared behind the bathroom door.

He wanted to go to her and thank her, but instead he began to dial. He might as well get this over with.

Ten minutes later Andi emerged from the bathroom. He didn't want to examine the way his heart bloomed in his chest when he saw her, so he busied himself closing the computer.

"Mac is making the arrangements right now. He assured me that we'd have a team at the meeting site tonight, ready to intercept El Diablo and the other two dealers. He said he wouldn't tell Olasik anything about it."

"Thank goodness," she said quietly. "How did the conversation go otherwise?"

Three days ago he would have given her a flip answer and moved on to a different subject. Now he said, "It went well. We didn't talk about what happened before or Richard's death. Mac asked me how my business was doing and apologized for tricking me into coming down here." He flashed her a grin. "I told him I'd accept his apology because it worked out okay and because he was going to be paying me a big chunk of money when it was over."

"I know how hard it must have been for you to call," she said.

He shrugged. "It was time. There are things you have to let go or they'll eat away at you forever."

She cocked her head to the side. "What other things do you have to let go of, Chase?"

He slid off the bed. "This computer, for one. We need to get going if we're going to make that appointment at the orphanage." He wasn't ready to tell her about his childhood.

She stared at him for a moment, then nodded. "I'll

just need a moment to dress. Are you sure it's safe to go outside?''

"I think so. I'm going to take a look around while you dress and get Paolo ready. But there are enough people on the street that I think we'll be able to blend in.''

In twenty minutes they were standing on the street in front of the hotel. Chase felt Andi's hesitation and glanced at her. She was looking at the crowds swirling around her, apprehension on her face.

"It's a lot of people after living in Chipultipe for so long, isn't it?'' he murmured. He put his hand at her waist. "Let's start walking. The orphanage isn't far.''

It took them only fifteen minutes. The orphanage was an old building that appeared lovingly cared for. When they rang the doorbell, a smiling nun opened the door to them.

"Señor Remington? We've been expecting you.''

Chase turned to Andi. "This is Andi McGinnis, Sister. And Paolo.''

"Come in. Let me show you around.''

The nun reached out and touched Paolo's face. "Is this the poor youngster who lost his mother recently?''

Andi nodded. Chase saw her hands whiten as she clutched Paolo to her chest.

As the nun gave them a tour of the orphanage, Chase kept glancing at Andi's face. All the children were clean and looked healthy. The older children played in groups in several small rooms, and Andi smiled at them. But as they walked through large rooms with rows and rows of cribs, each with a baby in it, he saw that she held Paolo more closely.

When they had returned to the foyer, Andi gave the nun a tight smile. "Thank you for showing us around, Sister. We appreciate it."

"We'd take good care of Paolo," the nun said gently.

"The children do seem happy," Andi finally answered.

"Some of them are adopted. For the rest, we try to make them feel like this is their home." The nun looked at a group of children walking by. "This is the only life they know, and they are content."

Andi nodded jerkily, her eyes bleak. "Thank you again, Sister. We'll let you know."

Chase guided her outside. When the door closed behind them, Andi took a deep shuddering breath and said fiercely, "I won't leave him there."

Chase put his arm around her shoulders and turned her toward their hotel. "Let's wait until we're back in the room to discuss it," he said. "We need to keep our eyes open and our attention on what's going on out here."

She nodded blindly and didn't say anything more as they made their way through the streets of Monterez. He tried to watch what was going on around them, but he was too worried about Andi to pay more than cursory attention.

When they were finally back in the hotel room,

Chase locked the door, then turned to her. "What's wrong, Andi?"

"I'm not leaving Paolo in that place."

She still held the baby tightly. "Why don't you put him down?" he suggested mildly. "I'm not sure he can breathe."

Andi looked down at the baby, who was squashed against her chest. Her hands loosened, and she set him on the blanket on the floor. "Did you see all those babies in cribs?" she asked, shuddering. "Just lying there, staring at the ceiling?"

"Those babies are probably better off in those cribs by themselves than they were before," he said, turning to watch Paolo on the floor. "You don't know their circumstances. At least with the nuns they're getting regular meals and some attention. They might be on the street otherwise. Or worse."

"I couldn't do that to Paolo. Or to Paloma. I promised her I would take care of him."

"Then what are you going to do, Andi?" He turned back to look at her, shoving his hands into his pockets. He didn't want to go to her, to touch her. He was feeling too vulnerable right now.

"I'll adopt him myself," she said slowly, her face lighting up and the tension falling away as she looked at Paolo. "He doesn't have anyone else, so I'll be his family."

"Don't make a rash decision," he warned.

Andi turned back to him, her face full of determination. And joy. "It's not a rash decision. It's absolutely the right thing to do. And I think it's been in the back of my mind all along. As soon as I said it, I knew it was what I wanted.''

He couldn't resist going to her and taking her in his arms. ''He'll be lucky to have you. Not all kids are as lucky as that.''

She must have heard something in his voice, because she leaned back and stared at him. ''You were one of those kids, weren't you, Chase?'' she asked softly. ''There was no one for you.''

For a moment he wanted to deny it, to brush her off with a quick remark and change the subject. But as he stared at her, something shifted inside him. He wanted to tell her about himself. And he saw in her eyes that she wanted to know.

''I wasn't an orphan, but I might as well have been,'' he said in a low voice. ''My dad took off before I was three. I never saw him again. My mother couldn't handle it, so she started to drink. By the time I was ten or twelve, she had a serious problem. She was pretty much drunk all the time, and I ran wild.

''But no one wanted to get involved. We lived in New York, so it was easy for me to hide. And it was easy for the neighbors to ignore us, tell themselves that someone else would surely bring the matter to the attention of the authorities. I managed to stay out of jail until I turned eighteen, then I took off and joined the army. My mother died a couple years later and I've never been back.''

She moved to him and slid her arms around him. ''It doesn't sound like there was much to go back for.

I'm sorry,'' she murmured. ''No one should have to
grow up like that.''

''I was lucky,'' he said. ''The army became my
family. I trained as a ranger, then the agency recruited
me. I finally felt like I'd found my place.''

''And then Mac sent me to spy on you,'' she whispered. ''No wonder you were angry when you found
out. You must have felt so betrayed.''

''I've had better days.'' His mouth curved up in a
humorless smile. ''I guess it felt like history repeating
itself.'' .

''That's exactly what it was. No one has ever been
there for you, have they? When the chips were down,
everyone has always walked away.''

He shrugged. ''I've managed to do okay on my
own.''

''You can't live that way for the rest of your life.''

''It's worked pretty well so far,'' he said.

''Don't you want a family someday?''

''What do I know about families?'' he asked.
''Nothing, except what they shouldn't be. I don't
know a damn thing about how kids should be raised.''

''I think you know quite a bit. If nothing else, you
know what not to do with kids. Look at Paolo. You've
done a great job with him.''

''I haven't had any choice.''

Her mouth curved up in a gentle smile. ''I think
it's that way with your own kids. You just kind of
jump in and do it.''

''Sort of like what you're doing with Paolo?''

"I guess it is. I don't know anything about kids, either. I just know I can't bear to leave him."

"If you're serious, we can talk to someone at the agency. They should be able to cut through all the red tape that would be required for adoption." He gathered her close, skimming a kiss over the top of her head. It had felt right to tell Andi about his past, about who he really was. A small part of him, a part that he thought had died long ago, was beginning to stir. There was a light at the corners of his life now, a light that was struggling to get in. He cautiously opened the door for it, just a crack.

"Thank you, Chase," Andi said, and she lifted her face to his. "You're not nearly as cold as you'd like everyone to think, are you?"

"No one has ever seen that but you," he answered. "Maybe you're seeing something that's not there."

Her mouth curled into a smile. "I don't think so. But if you're worried about your reputation, I promise I won't tell a soul."

His heart moved as he looked down at her, and he wanted to pull away. But instead he held her more tightly. How had he fallen for this woman? How had she snuck around the fence he'd erected around his heart? He'd done the one thing he'd always sworn he wouldn't do, and that was care about someone. Now he wasn't going to be able to forget about her after she left.

And leave she would. Andi was married to her job. She'd made that clear more than once. A small voice told him to ask her about it, ask her if she'd consider leaving her job to settle down, but he was afraid. Afraid he'd hear an answer he didn't want to hear.

So he pulled her close and kissed her, pushing the future firmly away. If all they had together were the next couple of days, he'd make the most of it. And if he'd let himself dream about things that wouldn't be, he'd pay the price after she left.

Andi snuggled closer to Chase, completely content. For the first time in days, it seemed, she didn't have something to do, somewhere to go. She had the precious gift of time, and she wanted to spend it exactly the way she was right now—with Chase.

His arm curled around her, pulling her closer, and she closed her eyes. Apparently Chase wanted to spend his time the same way. Paolo gurgled from his blanket on the floor, and she opened her eyes long enough to look down at him and smile. He was examining his toes and finding them perfectly fascinating.

Without thinking she grabbed Chase's hand. "Look at Paolo," she said. "He's figured out he has toes."

Chase leaned over her to look down at the baby. She saw the harsh lines on his face soften. "He's a smart kid, isn't he?"

"The smartest." She beamed at the baby. "And he's been so good during this trip."

"You've taken good care of him." Chase transferred his gaze to her, and his eyes warmed. "You've been wonderful with him, Andi," he said. "If you're really serious about adopting him, I think you'll make a great mother.''

"I'm very serious about adopting him." The more she thought about it, the more right it seemed. "As soon as this operation is over, I'm going to start the paperwork."

"I'd like to—"

He stopped in the middle of the sentence, his hand tightening on her arm. Then he picked up his gun from the nightstand.

"Take Paolo into the bathroom, then close the door and stay in there with him."

She was already moving off the bed. She'd heard the noise in the hall, too. "Do you think it's trouble?"

"I don't know, but I want the two of you out of the line of fire."

Andi scooped up Paolo and his blanket and hurried into the bathroom. She placed him on the floor, behind the porcelain base of the toilet. It was the most protected spot she could find. Then she closed the door behind him and moved back into the room to pick up her gun.

"I told you to stay in there with him." Chase's harsh whisper filled the room.

"I don't need to be protected," she said. "I'm not about to cower in the bathroom. What do you want me to do?"

He scowled at her, his face tight with anger. The furtive sound in the hall came again, closer to their room. He glanced at the door, then back at her. She saw the resignation in his face.

He gestured to the other side of the bed. "Stay over there and out of sight. We'll let him come barreling into the room, then try to grab him. I'd rather not kill him if we don't have to. I want to know who sent him."

She nodded and positioned herself on the floor, out of sight of the door to the room. Chase was still between her and the door, crouching behind the dresser, but at least he wasn't alone in the room. It wouldn't take long for a gunman to find either of them, but if the room appeared empty, maybe it would buy them enough time to surprise an intruder.

The silence filled her head, magnifying the slightest sound from the room and the hall. She heard Paolo babbling happily to himself in the bathroom. From the hall she heard the soft whisper of footsteps, moving much too slowly for anyone with legitimate business in the hotel. The sounds were almost at their door now. She imagined she could hear a muffled click as the person in the hall checked his gun one last time.

She glanced at Chase and saw that he was watching her. She gave him a thumb's-up and a smile, and he nodded at her. Then he looked back at the door.

She'd seen worry on his face. Didn't he believe she was capable of dealing with the threat? Or was he concerned about her personally? She hoped it was the latter, but she wasn't sure. In the past several days she'd allowed herself to care about Chase, to hope they had some kind of a future together, but she had no idea how he felt about her.

He'd told her he had nothing to offer her, and

maybe he'd told her no more than the truth. She gripped her gun more tightly and stared at the door as her heart contracted with pain.

Don't think about that now, she ordered herself fiercely. She forced herself to put Chase out of her mind, to think about nothing but the approaching threat.

She heard the quiet click of the lock opening, then the door handle began to turn, slowly and silently. She looked over at Chase and found him watching it, too. He glanced at her and nodded, and she shifted the gun in her hand.

When the door began to ease open, she lowered herself to the floor. The space between the floor and the bottom of the bed allowed her to see the first foot or so of the room door. She saw the darkness of the hall and felt the current of air that swept through the room from the hall, but she didn't move. Chase was still and silent, too.

She watched a pair of feet clad in military-style boots step cautiously into the room, then hesitate. The man had probably expected to surprise her and Chase, and he was now wondering where they'd gone. In the intruder's moment of indecision, Chase acted.

He swept out one leg and the man fell heavily to the floor. Instantly Chase was on top of him, holding his gun to the man's head. Andi scrambled to her feet and moved around the bed to Chase's side.

He never took his eyes off the intruder. "Cover him," he said curtly. "I'm going to search him."

"Got it." She squatted on the floor, holding her

gun steadily to the man's head. Out of the corner of her eye, she saw Chase thoroughly searching him.

In a few minutes Chase stood up. He held another gun and two knives in his hands. "He meant business," he said grimly.

Andi looked back at their captive. "What now?"

"You keep your gun on him. I'm going to tie him up."

In a matter of seconds Chase had removed the man's belt and tied his hands firmly behind his back. Then he cut off a piece of the man's shirt and tied his feet together. Finally he turned the man over so they could study his face.

Andi trained her gun on him, as did Chase. The man had a mustache, dirty unkempt hair and nondescript clothes. His boots were the only thing out of the ordinary about him. They looked like U.S. military surplus, and new.

"Who are you?" Chase asked in Spanish.

The man stared at him insolently, then spit out of the corner of his mouth.

Chase looked at him for a moment, his face hard and cold. Andi wondered what he was thinking.

"Move away from him," Chase said without looking at her. "But don't put your gun away."

She wondered what he was doing even as she did as he asked.

Chase shoved his gun into the man's groin. The intruder's eyes opened wide, and the insolence disappeared from his face. It was replaced by fear.

"It looks like we've found a language you understand," Chase said grimly. "Who are you?"

The man muttered a name.

"All right, Mr. Santangelo. Now we're making progress. Who sent you here?"

Sweat sheened the man's forehead, and he looked frantically at the gun pushed into his groin. He muttered something else, too low for Andi to hear, and Chase shook his head.

"Sorry, Santangelo, being too frightened to tell me isn't an option. You've got two choices right now. You can tell me who sent you, or you can lose a vital portion of your anatomy." Chase gave him a grim smile and cocked the hammer on his gun. "Which is it going to be?"

The man closed his eyes as sweat poured down his face. Andi watched silently. He would give them the name, she knew. It was only a matter of how long it took.

Finally the man started shaking, then he spat out a name. It was El Diablo.

Chase nodded and pulled his gun away. "I knew you would make the right decision, Santangelo. Now, how long is your buddy going to wait before he comes up?"

Andi saw the start of surprise in the man's eyes. His gaze darted to the door, and Chase smiled again. "No, he's not going to save you. He's going to join you."

He shoved his gun into the waistband of his pants and dragged their captive to the other side of the bed.

Then he turned to Andi. "If he makes a sound, shoot him."

"Right."

She knelt next to him and pressed her gun into his head, staring at him with stone-cold eyes. He needed to think she wouldn't hesitate to shoot him.

Chase eased closed the door of the room, and they waited again. Her captive was sweating, and the acrid smell filled the room. It wasn't long before they heard footsteps again.

The scene was repeated with the second intruder, and it took only a minute for Chase to search, then tie up the second man. He, too, was dressed in non-descript clothing, with the exception of the boots.

When both men were tied up and lying next to each other, Chase asked, "How many more are out there?"

The first man answered quickly, "There was only the two of us."

Chase stared at them for a while, then looked over at Andi. "Do you think he's telling the truth?"

She studied the men. The second one was still defiant, but the first man was terrified. She could smell his fear. "I think so." She glanced up at him. "But you might want to question him again."

Before Chase could bend down, the first man sobbed, "No, no. I am telling the truth. There is no one else."

Chase stared down at the men as the silence stretched out. Then he looked over at Andi. "Assuming we believe him, what are we going to do with them?"

Andi knew how the game was played. She gave Chase a bored look. "The easiest thing to do would be to shoot them. Then we wouldn't have to worry about them. What do you think?"

Some of the insolence drained from the face of the second man, and he began to look uneasy.

Chase studied their captives for a moment, then said, "I don't know. Maybe they can be useful."

"I don't see how. They don't have any information to give us. I say get rid of them."

Chase pointed his gun at the first man and tightened his finger on the trigger. "If you say so."

"No, wait, *Señor!*" the first man cried. "We have much information to give you."

Chase pretended to consider. "What do you think?" he asked Andi.

Andi shrugged. "I suppose it wouldn't hurt to hear what they have to say. Then we can decide if it's worthwhile." The look she gave the two men said she doubted it would be.

Chase stared at the men for a long moment, then slowly put the safety back on his gun. "Okay, fellows. Let's hear what you have to say. And it better be worthwhile. My partner has a very quick temper."

Chapter 14

An hour later Andi, with Paolo in his sling against her chest, stood next to Chase outside the hotel room. They listened at the door for a long time, but didn't hear any sounds from the room. Finally Chase nodded at her and they moved silently down the hallway.

They'd fallen into a natural rhythm as they questioned the two thugs, like partners who had worked together for years. Now they moved together, each knowing instinctively what the other would do.

When they reached the entrance to the hotel, they paused, scanning the street. After what seemed like a long time, Chase said in a low voice, "I don't see anyone suspicious. How about you?"

"Everything looks clear."

"Okay, then, let's go. We're going to walk around

until we're both satisfied we're not being followed. Then we'll stop at the first place that looks promising."

They had left their two intruders bound, gagged and blindfolded in the room, along with the radio transmitter they'd found hidden in the computer case. Chase's face had gone grim and hard when they'd found it, but they hadn't said anything in front of the two thugs. Now they just needed to get away and find a new place to hide.

After walking around Monterez for a couple of hours and making sure they weren't being followed, they found another hotel that was even shabbier and more run-down than the first, the kind where the desk clerk didn't ask, or answer, any questions. After they checked into a room, Andi fed Paolo while Chase went through the computer, the case and the cell phone one more time, even though he'd checked them all earlier.

"It looks like that was the only bug," he finally said.

"It had to be Olasik," she said.

"Looks that way. I didn't talk to or deal with anyone but him. And he's the one who made the appointment at the orphanage, which is where those two clowns were apparently waiting for us."

"I'm sorry, Chase," she said as she fed Paolo. "If I hadn't gotten so upset at the orphanage, we both would have been more alert and might have noticed those two following us."

"Don't worry about it. It turned out okay. We even got some useful information from them."

"Olasik must be the American in El Diablo's pay that those two thugs were talking about," she said.

Chase nodded. "No wonder we've had such a hard time catching the guy. Something has gone wrong with every operation we've run against him."

"We need to call Mac and let him know."

Chase nodded again. "I've already told him not to say anything to Olasik about the plan for tonight. Something about the guy bothered me. But maybe Mac can set up a little sting operation to catch Olasik himself. He's been after him for years, and now we know who he is." He picked up the secure cell phone and began punching in the number to Mac's pager.

"I'd like to talk to Mac when you get hold of him," Andi said.

Something flickered in Chase's eyes. He punched in the last number, then closed the phone. "All right. Can I ask what you want to talk to him about?"

"I want him to include me in that operation tonight. I want to be there when they capture El Diablo."

Chase stared at her and felt his face grow cold, echoing the coldness that settled around his heart. For a long time he couldn't say a thing. Finally he cleared his throat.

"I'm not sure that's such a good idea, Andi. You just finished a grueling trek through the jungle, and you need to take some time off before you start another job. You know the agency regulations."

He tried to keep his voice neutral and his face carefully blank. But his heart was crumbling.

She didn't look at him. "This isn't a new job," she said, a defiant tone in her voice. "It's the culmination of this one. And I want to be there when it's finished."

"Look at you, Andi. You're worn-out. You've been on the move through rough terrain for four days, and last night was the first decent night's sleep you got. Why would you want to go on a dangerous mission like capturing El Diablo and risk getting hurt because you weren't one hundred percent?"

"I have to do it." She clamped her lips together and turned her back to him. "Don't you understand? The time I spent in Chipultipe, Paloma's life, it was all to catch El Diablo. How can I sit on the sidelines now?"

"Mac will make sure the agents he sends are the best," Chase said, watching the tension in her spine, seeing the urgency vibrating from her body. As he watched her, he felt his dreams dissolve and disappear. "El Diablo will be captured whether you're there or not."

She spun around to face him. "I have to be there, Chase. I have to be."

He'd been a fool. Jumping off the bed, he went to the grimy window that was barely covered by a dirty set of curtains. He stared blindly through the crack in the curtains onto the street below. He'd begun to hope that Andi felt something for him, that she would be willing to give up this life and make a new life with him and Paolo. Now every word she spoke was a club, dashing his hopes into tiny pieces.

"Why do you have to be there, Andi?" he asked quietly.

"Because I do." He heard the hesitation in her voice and turned around to look at her. Her face was full of anguish.

His head told him to back away, to let her go. She would never have stayed, anyway. But his heart made him go to her, to take her hand. "Tell me."

Her hand tightened in his, and he thought she was going to pull away. Then she sighed. "Let's sit down. This could take a while."

The pain in his chest eased just a little. At least she trusted him enough to tell him why it was so important to her. He was willing to bet she wouldn't have told him four days ago.

"What's going on, Andi?"

She pulled her legs close to her body and wrapped her arms around them, staring into the distance. "Do you remember the bombing of the U.S. Embassy in the Middle East twelve years ago? It got a lot of coverage at the time."

He frowned. "I remember it. But I've forgotten the details."

"Twenty-five people were killed and more than a hundred injured. The bombing was the work of an unnamed terrorist who was working for one of the fundamentalist groups in that area."

He nodded. "Yeah, that's right."

"My parents were two of the people killed in that bombing."

"Hell, Andi. I'm sorry." He wanted to reach out and hold her, but he didn't move. She was cocooned in a world of her own. "I didn't know."

"Not too many people do." She glanced at him. "I was sixteen years old and at school in the States. That's the only reason I wasn't killed, too."

"What does that have to do with El Diablo?"

She gave him a thin smile. "El Diablo is the terrorist who was responsible for the bombing."

He frowned at her. "How can you be sure of that?"

"After my parents were killed, I found out everything I could about the embassy attack. Because I was one of the victims, I was allowed access to some of the classified documents. I was able to follow the trail back to El Diablo."

"What was a drug dealer doing working for terrorists?"

"He started dealing drugs to pay for his terrorist work. That was in his religious phase." Her eyes were dark with loathing. "Then I guess he had another conversion. He realized that he liked having money and the power that went with it. So he got out of terrorism and into the drug business full-time. That's when he became El Diablo."

"Does the government know this?"

"I'm sure they do. I got all my information from government documents."

"So catching El Diablo is personal for you," he said quietly.

"You're damn right it is." She turned to him angrily. "That monster killed my parents and twenty-three other innocent people, and maimed dozens more. That was just in that one attack. The government thinks he's responsible for a number of other attacks in that region that killed a lot of other people. Of course I want to catch him."

"But you're not objective about this case. You want more than justice, Andi. You want revenge."

She sprang off the bed and paced the room. "I stood at my parents' grave and promised them that whoever was responsible would be caught. I call that justice, not revenge."

"Sometimes, if everything works out, the best revenge is justice, but you're never going to be able to see clearly when you're personally involved. You should know that by now."

"All I know is that we're close to catching that monster, and I have to be there."

He wanted to ask her if she was making her choice between her job and him, but he already knew the answer. There wasn't any choice. Andi had already chosen her job.

"What about Paolo?" he asked, trying to find a way to make her stop and think.

"What about him?"

"I thought you wanted to adopt him."

"I do. And I will."

"What if you're killed during this operation? What will he do then?"

Her face paled, but the determination there never

wavered. "I'm not going to be killed. El Diablo has no idea that we know about the new meeting site. He's expecting us to go to the place Paloma told us about."

"You can't be sure of that," he said.

"I'm not going to be killed."

"What are you going to do when El Diablo is captured, Andi?" he asked softly. "Are you going to shoot him yourself? Is that how you're going to take your revenge?"

"Of course not!" She whirled to face him again. "My revenge is going to be watching him sit and rot in prison for the rest of his life. That would be justice. And that's what I'm going to get."

"You don't have to do it yourself, though. Let Mac put a team of agents in there to capture him. Stay here with Paolo." *And me.* "El Diablo will still be caught and punished, even if you're not there."

"I can't do that, Chase," she said, and he saw the anguish on her face again. "Don't you understand? I made a promise at my parents' grave that I would catch this man, and I have to do it. Then I can adopt Paolo and get on with my life."

"What is it you want from the rest of your life?" he asked.

For the first time he saw uncertainty in her face. "I'm not sure. I've always been so focused on catching El Diablo. I've never thought about what would happen after that."

"Maybe you better think about it."

Hell, why did it have to be Andi? Why did it have

to be a woman who was so complicated? Why couldn't he have found some nice ordinary woman to fall in love with?

He froze when the words passed through his mind. He wasn't in love with Andi. He scrambled to deny it. He might be in lust with her, he might want to continue seeing her when they were finished with this job, but he wasn't in love with her.

He wasn't ever going to fall in love.

His denials sounded weak and futile, and his heart laughed at him. He stared at Andi and the certainty of his feelings stared back at him. *He loved her.*

"Can't you understand, Chase?" Her voice was low and tortured. "I *have* to do this. I couldn't live with myself if I didn't."

And because he loved her, he saw that she was right. Because of who Andi was, she needed to be present at the capture of El Diablo. She had made a promise and she would keep it.

He leaned against the wall and closed his eyes. "Yeah, Andi, I do understand. I know you have to do it. I just don't want you to do it."

"Why not, Chase?"

He opened his eyes and stared at her. "I don't want you to get hurt. Is that so tough to understand?"

Tentatively she moved closer to him and he finally gave in to the need inside him and wrapped his arms around her. "I...care about you, Andi."

It was all he could bring himself to say to her. He held his breath, waiting for a response.

She burrowed closer to him. "And I care about you, Chase. I knew you would understand."

He had to make a choice. Did he tell Andi to go, to find her revenge for her parents? Or did he ask her to stay?

He was damned either way. If he asked her to stay, after she was so clear on her need to go, it would irreparably damage their relationship. But if she went, she might not come back. And she would be just one more person who'd left him.

But she would leave a much bigger hole in his heart than any of the others.

He had no choice. Not really. So he tightened his arms around her and said, "I'll tell Mac when he calls that you want to be part of the team."

She lifted her face and he saw the joy and relief there. "Thank you, Chase."

A small ugly voice inside his head told him this was a test. When push came to shove, would she really go? Would she choose her job over him? He tried to banish the thought, but it wouldn't disappear.

Maybe this was his test, too. Could he let Andi go, let her do what she had to do? He wasn't sure, and he prayed that Mac wouldn't call, that she wouldn't have to make the choice. And neither would he.

"I'll take care of Paolo while you're gone tonight," he said, glancing over to where the baby slept.

"Thank you," she said. "I know he'll be fine with you."

"I've never watched him by myself," he warned.

"You've always been there to make sure I didn't mess up."

"You'll be fine. You've taken care of him a lot on this trip. You know what to do for him."

He smiled. "Who would have thought I'd end up watching the kid while I let a woman go on the mission?"

Her eyes glowed. "I'd say you've come a long way, Chase."

He wanted to tell her that it was because of her; only his love for her would have kept him in this room while she walked into danger. But he couldn't do it. He couldn't confess his feelings. It was too risky. A chance he wasn't ready to take.

"Why don't you take a nap?" he said. "You're probably not going to get much sleep tonight."

"I can't sleep. I'm too excited."

He watched as she paced the room, pausing only to peer outside through the crack in the curtains. His stomach clenched. He wanted her to say she would stay with him. He wanted her to say he was more important than her revenge.

But she had carried her promise to her parents in her heart for years. He would try to understand. And she would never know that in his heart he prayed she would change her mind.

Before he could say anything else to her, the cellular phone rang. Andi spun around and stared at him, her face tense. He picked up the phone and said, "Yeah?"

"Chase?"

"Hello, Mac."

"What's up?"

Quickly Chase told Mac what had happened with the two intruders in their room, and how they suspected that Olasik was the traitor in the agency. "Thank God you and McGinnis are all right," Mac said. Chase could hear the controlled anger in his voice. "And I think we can plan a little something for Olasik."

Chase hesitated. "What did you tell him about tonight?"

"I told him everything was set—for the original meeting place. I didn't say anything about the change."

"Thank God. I knew there was something off about him."

"You always did have good instincts." Chase heard the wistful tone in Mac's voice. "I was damn sorry when you left the agency."

Chase knew it was the closest Mac would ever come to an apology. "It was time for me to leave," he said gruffly. "I needed to get on with my life."

And that was the closest he would ever come to telling Mac it was okay.

Mac cleared his throat. "I'm going to set up a little surprise for Olasik at the original meeting place," he said. "I have a feeling that Olasik will go out there to collect his reward from El Diablo for his information. We'll have someone there waiting for him."

"Good idea," Chase said. "I was going to suggest the same thing."

"We're all set with the team for tonight," Mac continued. "I'll call you and McGinnis and let you know as soon as we get El Diablo."

"You're not quite set," Chase said. "Andi wants to be part of the team."

There was silence on the other end of the phone. Finally Mac said, "Is she in shape to take part?"

"She thinks she is. This is her mission. She's the one who set this up. She has the right to be there if she wants to be."

Chase glanced at Andi, willing her to change her mind. Willing her to say she wanted to stay with him. But she didn't say a thing.

"All right." Mac's voice was abrupt. "Tell her to be in front of the main post office in Monterez in two hours. I'll have someone pick her up."

They disconnected, and Chase listened to the dial tone for a moment before he closed the phone. He looked over at Andi. "You're on. You need to be at the main post office in two hours. Someone will pick you up."

She licked her lips and nodded. "I'll be there."

Chapter 15

Andi looked at Chase and she saw the resignation on his face. And she saw the shadow of pain, deep in his eyes. Then, with a flash of insight, she realized what she was doing to him.

He had told her he cared about her. For Chase, that was a huge admission. She knew how hard it had been for him to say even that. He might never be able to give her more. But she knew without a doubt that his feelings for her ran deep.

He would never have agreed to let her go on the mission if they didn't. Chase was a hard, tough man. It would go against all his instincts to let a woman he cared about walk into danger. There was only one reason he would have agreed—because he saw how important it was to her.

But what was it doing to him? It had to be a bitter betrayal. She had become just one more person who was leaving him, one more person who wasn't there when he needed her.

"Chase." She said only his name, but suddenly he was all that mattered.

He stood. "You'd better get ready," he said gruffly. "We'll have to leave soon to get you to the post office on time and make sure no one follows us."

Without taking her eyes off him she slowly shook her head. "I'm not going."

He stared at her as if he hadn't heard her correctly. "What?"

"I said I'm not going. I can't."

He grabbed her hands and held on tightly. "Why not?"

She saw the faint light of hope in his eyes and damned herself for almost extinguishing it. "Everyone has always left you when you needed them, Chase. Everyone. I can't be another person who leaves you."

"You'll come back."

"Yes, I would have come back. But it doesn't matter now. This time I'm not leaving. I'm going to stay with you."

"You just told me how important this is to you. How it's defined your life for the past twelve years. And you're going to give it up just like that?"

"Yes, I am. There are some things that are more important."

"Like what?" She thought he held his breath.

"Like you, Chase." She, too, held her breath. She was taking a chance. She was exposing herself, telling Chase she cared about him, loved him. She was completely vulnerable, taking the risk of being horribly hurt if Chase rejected her. She was opening herself to the possibility of searing pain.

But somehow that didn't matter. Chase needed to know she would be there for him. He needed to know she wasn't going to be another person who left him, another person who put other people, other events, before him. Chase needed to know he would always come first with her.

"Are you sure?" he whispered.

She nodded. "Positive."

He picked up the phone and dialed again, punching in the number of Mac's pager without taking his eyes off her. When he closed the phone, the tiny click echoed loudly in the silent room, almost as loudly as the pounding of her heart. This was when Chase was supposed to say he loved her, and she was supposed to say she loved him, too. This was where happily ever after was supposed to begin.

He didn't say a word.

Her pulse roared in her ears and she felt the chill of uneasiness steal into her bones. *Please, Chase,* she wanted to beg, *say something. Anything.*

But he was silent, holding the phone tightly in one hand, staring at her. She wanted to throw herself into his arms, beg him to say the right words, tell her she hadn't made a total fool of herself.

Then Paolo let out a piercing wail, and she whirled

to him, grateful for the interruption. Taking care of Paolo would give both her and Chase a chance to regain their equilibrium.

"I'll run the bottle under some hot water to heat it up," Chase said, and he disappeared in the small grimy bathroom.

A few minutes later he came out and handed her the warm bottle. She'd been walking the room with Paolo at her shoulder, murmuring to him while he chewed on his fist. When she offered him the bottle, he settled down to eat greedily.

Avoiding Chase's eyes, she sat on the bed and leaned against the wall. Even though she wasn't looking at him, she could feel Chase's gaze on her. Finally she looked up and met his eyes, bracing herself for the pain.

"You don't have to say anything." She forced the words out of her mouth, even though her throat felt swollen and tight. "It's all right."

He shook his head. "You don't understand. It's not what you think."

"Then what is it?" She kept her gaze deliberately blank, when all she wanted was to curl into herself and howl with pain.

Before he could answer, the cellular phone chirped again. He opened it and said, "Yeah?"

He gripped the phone tightly as he said, "She's not going, Mac. She changed her mind."

He listened for what seemed like a long time. Then he said, "You'll have to ask her sometime. But she's busy right now. Call us as soon as you have some information.''

He listened for another few seconds, then snapped the phone shut again. Then he looked over at her. ''Mac wants to know why you changed your mind.''

''Why didn't you tell him?''

To her surprise a faint wash of color crept into his cheeks. ''It wasn't any of his damn business. You can tell him what you want, but I wasn't about to fill him in on my personal life.''

''Am I part of that personal life?'' The words came out stiffly. She hoped he didn't hear the fear behind them.

He gave her an incredulous look. ''What do you think, Andi?''

''I think you've gotten awfully quiet since I said I wouldn't go on the operation tonight.'' She shifted on the bed. Paolo had fallen asleep, become a dead weight in her arms. ''I wasn't trying to force anything on you or trap you in any way. I was just telling you how I felt.''

Chase eased onto the bed next to her. He looked down at the sleeping Paolo, then eased the baby out of her arms. He held him for a moment, gazing down at his face, and an expression of love and tenderness softened his features. Then, very carefully, he got off the bed and put the baby into his makeshift crib.

He sat down close to Andi and took her hand in his. ''I didn't think you were trying to trap me or force me into anything. That's not why I didn't say anything.''

He gripped her hand tightly, and she turned her palm so that it was pressing against his. "Why, then, Chase?" she whispered.

"I couldn't say anything. I was too ashamed."

"Ashamed?" She frowned.

He nodded and pulled her closer, his free hand coming up to brush her hair away from her face. "I didn't want you to go. I was really angry at first when you said you needed to be there tonight. Then you told me about your parents, and I understood why you felt you had to be there. But I still didn't want you to go. I was worried about you and worried about Paolo."

He swallowed once, and she watched the ripple of muscle down his throat. He took her other hand and twined their fingers together. "But I knew I couldn't stop you. Worse, I knew it would be wrong to stop you. This was something you needed to do. I could see that, but I still didn't want you to go. So I gave you a test. I told you to go, hoping you would stay. A part of me said that if you cared about me enough, you would choose to stay. And now I'm ashamed of that."

Her heart cracked open and tumbled into his hands. "Oh, Chase, you have nothing to be ashamed about."

"Yes, I do. I didn't trust you enough to do the right thing. The right thing for you."

"Has anyone ever cared about doing the right thing for you?"

He scowled. "That's not the point."

"That's exactly the point. Trusting someone else

completely is a huge step. And for someone who's never had the security of unconditional love, it's very hard. Of course you weren't sure what I would do. And of course you wanted me to choose to stay with you. There's nothing wrong with that.''

His hands tightened almost painfully on hers. ''You're not angry that I was testing you?''

''Of course not.'' She gave him a blinding smile as a huge weight lifted off her chest. ''I'm sure there will be times when I'll test you, too. But it doesn't mean I don't...care about you.'' She was afraid to tell him she loved him, afraid he wasn't ready to hear the words.

He gazed at her, his eyes filled with a light she'd never seen before, then pulled her into his arms. ''Andi, I love you,'' he whispered. ''I've never said that to any other woman. I never intended to say it to a woman. But you snuck around all my defenses. When I thought about you going on that operation tonight, still exhausted from our trip through the jungle, I was frantic. I couldn't bear the thought of losing you.''

''That's why I'm not going,'' she said. ''I was only thinking of myself, of what I needed. I hadn't thought at all about what you needed. And when I realized how much I was hurting you by insisting on going, I couldn't do it.''

She leaned back and grasped his arms. ''I love you, too, Chase. You're more important to me than revenge. El Diablo will end up in jail and that's all that matters. I suddenly realized that it wasn't important to me anymore to do it personally. You are the most important thing in my life now. You and Paolo.''

They both glanced at the sleeping baby, and Chase said, ''Yeah, the little squirt kind of grows on you, doesn't he?''

''You're crazy about him, too. Don't try to hide it. I've seen the way you talk to him when you think no one's looking,'' she teased. ''He's got you wrapped firmly around his little finger.''

''He's not the only one.'' He framed her face with his hands and kissed her, and her heart moved in her chest at his tenderness. ''A certain woman agent has me completely in her power.''

''Is that so?'' She smiled against his lips. ''Does that mean you'll do whatever I say?''

''Try me.''

She murmured a suggestion into his ear, and he leaned back and gave her a slow, hot smile. ''I like the way your mind works,'' he said, his voice husky. ''I like it very much.''

He pressed her back onto the bed and leaned over her. He didn't kiss her, though. He lightly framed her face with his hands, letting his thumbs caress her cheeks.

''You mean everything to me,'' he said. But beneath the passion that filled his eyes she saw the uncertainty, the last vestige of doubt. And she realized that it would take a long time to remove every trace of doubt from Chase's eyes. He'd been alone in the world for far too long.

"I love you," she answered, wrapping her arms around his neck. "I'll always love you."

And she would. He was the other part of her, the part that was missing. She'd felt it three years ago, but wouldn't allow herself to act on it then. Now she would make sure she told him so every day.

Need sparked in his eyes, hot and intense. When she pulled him down to her, the tenderness and love in his kiss squeezed her heart. She opened herself to him, holding nothing back, giving him all the love in her heart.

Their clothes disappeared, removed by trembling hands. When they were naked, she twined herself around him, wanting to feel the touch of his skin everywhere, wanting the taste and feel of Chase to surround her and fill her.

He murmured her name as he caressed her, his hands gliding from her face to her breasts to her belly. Passion and need flared inside her.

"I can't wait any longer," she whispered. "I need to feel you inside me."

He groaned as he joined them together. She reached for his hands and twined her fingers with his. "Open your eyes," he said. "Look at me."

She opened her eyes to see him. All the doubt, all the pain was gone from his face. There was only his love, shining steadily down at her.

As they watched each other, murmuring words of love, her body tensed and then shattered with her climax. His eyes darkened and then he, too, shuddered and found his release.

He kissed her, a long deep kiss that joined their souls. And when he pulled her close and cradled her next to his body, she finally closed her eyes. She and Chase were together, and that was all that mattered.

The chirping noise dragged Andi from the depths of sleep. Then the heat and comfort of Chase's body moved away, and she opened her eyes abruptly. He was reaching for the cellular phone.

"Yeah?"

He listened for a long time, and she saw his face harden again. He looked like the Chase who had come to Chipultipe, a hard distant man.

"Thanks, Mac," he finally said, then snapped the phone closed.

He pulled her close again. "They caught Olasik. He was waiting at the original airstrip, just like we thought he would be."

"Did they get a confession out of him?"

"Not yet, but Mac doesn't think it'll take long. He's already gotten hold of Olasik's bank records, and he's got a lot of unexplained deposits. Olasik'll see the advantages of cooperating."

"Thank goodness they caught him," she said quietly. She paused, and she could feel Chase tense. "What about El Diablo?"

"Nothing yet. Agents are in place at the new airstrip, but so far, no sign of him or his buddies."

"There's still time."

"Yeah." He leaned away from her just enough to

see her face. "Are you sure you don't regret not going out to the airstrip?"

"I'm sure." She didn't hesitate. "You're far more important to me than catching El Diablo."

He touched her face again, then took her hand. Andi's heart moved again. She had no idea Chase could be so demonstrative. "I want to ask you a question, but I want to wait until after they catch him."

"Why do you want to wait?"

"Because your answer might depend on whether or not he shows up tonight."

Her heart began to pound. "I doubt it, Chase. I told you that you were more important than El Diablo, and I meant it." She held his gaze with her own. "Ask me now."

She saw the uncertainty in his eyes again, the wisp of fear. Then he cleared his throat. "Andi, will you marry me?"

Joy bubbled through her. "Of course I'll marry you, Chase. I love you. There's nothing I want more than to spend the rest of my life with you."

She saw the happiness well up inside him. "You're sure you don't want to wait until we find out if they catch El Diablo?"

"I'm positive. I've done my part to catch him. From now on it's up to someone else. You're stuck with me, I'm afraid. You're not going to get rid of me using a cheap trick like that."

"What about your job?" he asked, and she thought he held his breath.

"What about it? I only joined the agency because I wanted to catch El Diablo."

"You're good at your job, though," he said, watching her carefully. "Are you sure you want to give it up?"

"Are you trying to talk me out of marrying you?" she demanded. "Because it's not going to work." She grinned at him. "And besides, I hear there's a private-investigations agency in Denver that's recently come into a lot of money and is looking to hire a new associate. I don't come cheap, but I do good work."

Andi saw the tension drain out of him. "Thank God. I thought you might not want to leave the agency."

"My job with the agency is finished," she said quietly. "And even if it wasn't, you're far more important than a job. I couldn't bear to be separated from you for weeks or months at a time."

Chase closed his eyes and gathered her close. "I don't know anything about being a husband, Andi. But I swear I'll learn. You'll never regret marrying me."

"How could I ever regret marrying you? I love you. And we'll learn about marriage together. I'm sure I have a lot to learn about being a wife." She heard Paolo stirring and looked at Chase, who'd heard him, too.

"And I guess we're going to learn together how to be parents." She grasped his hands and asked, "Are you sure you don't mind? About Paolo, I mean? I can't leave him in an orphanage."

"I wouldn't let you." He kissed her again, then got up and took Paolo out of the dresser drawer. "I think I started thinking of him as my kid when he got sick. He's coming home with us." He gazed down at the baby, and Andi saw the love shining in his eyes.

"I didn't want to take this job," he continued, "but it's been the best thing that ever happened to me. I found everything that was missing in my life down here. You and Paolo complete me. You're the parts of me that have always been missing. I love you, Andi. And I love Paolo."

He smiled at her, and she saw only happiness in his eyes. All the shadows were gone, banished from his life. He took her hand and raised it to his lips. "Let's go home."

Epilogue

Paolo ran into the kitchen on his chubby two-year-old legs, his dark eyes gleaming, the dimple on his cheek flashing as he grinned at Andi. "Dada me," he called.

"That's right, buddy, Daddy's going to get you." Chase swooped into the room behind him, grabbed him and swung him into the air. The boy's shrieks of laughter blended with Chase's carefree chuckles.

Andi arched her back, trying to ease the ache, as she set the newspaper on the table and grinned at them. "I thought the idea was to settle him down so he would go to bed for his nap."

"We're settling down," Chase protested. He looked at Paolo. "Right, buddy? We're settling down right now."

Paolo nodded so vigorously that his shiny cap of black hair jumped on his forehead. ''Set down.''

Andi eased herself off the chair and gave Paolo a kiss as she hooked her arm around Chase's waist. ''Maybe we should call you Parrot, instead of Paolo.'' Her hand lingered on the child's head. ''You mimic everything your daddy says.''

''Dada,'' Paolo repeated.

Andi laughed and kissed Paolo again. ''Off to bed with you, sweetheart. Do you want Daddy to read you a story first?''

'''Tory!'' Paolo shouted.

Chase grinned at her. ''I learned my lesson yesterday. I promise I'll pick a nice soothing story to read to him.''

Andi watched them leave the room, Chase's dark-blond head bent close to Paolo's black one. After a few minutes she heard the low rumble of Chase's voice, punctuated occasionally by Paolo's high-pitched childish tone.

Finally there was silence, and in a few moments Chase walked back into the kitchen, crossed to Andi and bent down to give her a kiss. ''Paolo's asleep,'' he said. ''How's the rest of my family doing?''

Andi caught his hand and placed in on her protruding abdomen. ''Your second son must be planning a career as a soccer player. He's been practicing his kicks all day.''

Chase's hand lingered on her belly. She never got tired of seeing the awe on his face when he felt their baby move inside her. Then he leaned over and kissed her again.

"I saw the way you were stretching your back earlier. Do you want a rub?"

Her heart overflowed with love, and she gave Chase an intimate smile. "In a minute." She picked up the newspaper. "You need to look at this article first."

"What is it?"

"Read it."

She watched as he read the article, then put the paper back on the table. "It's finally over," he said quietly.

She nodded. "El Diablo has been sentenced to forty years in prison. And the prosecutor recommended that he serve eighty-five percent of his sentence before he can be considered for parole. He'll die in prison."

"He's going to pay for the deaths of your parents and Paloma and all the other people he killed."

Andi nodded and looked down at the newspaper, barely seeing the print through eyes suddenly swimming with tears. "We should save this article for Paolo," she whispered. "When he gets older, he'll want to know about his mother. We can show him that the man who killed her is in prison and won't ever get out."

"I'll add it to the collection," Chase replied. He took her hand and massaged her fingers. "Now, how about that back rub?"

She smiled up at him and put her hand in his. "Sounds like heaven."

Chase helped her out of the chair, then wrapped his arm around her as they headed toward the bedroom. They stopped at the door to Paolo's room to watch their son sleep.

"I'm a lucky man," Chase said.

Andi watched him and felt her heart overflow. "I love you, Chase Remington."

He turned and gave her the smile that always made her heart flutter. "And I love you, Mrs. Remington."

* * * * *

If you enjoyed what you just read,
then we've got an offer you can't resist!

Take 2 bestselling
love stories FREE!
Plus get a FREE surprise gift!

Clip this page and mail it to Silhouette Reader Service™

IN U.S.A.	IN CANADA
3010 Walden Ave.	P.O. Box 609
P.O. Box 1867	Fort Erie, Ontario
Buffalo, N.Y. 14240-1867	L2A 5X3

YES! Please send me 2 free Silhouette Intimate Moments® novels and my free surprise gift. Then send me 6 brand-new novels every month, which I will receive months before they're available in stores. In the U.S.A., bill me at the bargain price of $3.57 plus 25¢ delivery per book and applicable sales tax, if any*. In Canada, bill me at the bargain price of $3.96 plus 25¢ delivery per book and applicable taxes**. That's the complete price and a savings of over 10% off the cover prices—what a great deal! I understand that accepting the 2 free books and gift places me under no obligation ever to buy any books. I can always return a shipment and cancel at any time. Even if I never buy another book from Silhouette, the 2 free books and gift are mine to keep forever. So why not take us up on our invitation. You'll be glad you did!

245 SEN CNFF
345 SEN CNFG

Name	(PLEASE PRINT)	
Address	Apt.#	
City	State/Prov.	Zip/Postal Code

THOSE MARRYING McBRIDES!:

**The four *single* McBride siblings have always been
unlucky in love. But it looks as if their luck is
about to change....**

Rancher Joe McBride was a man who'd sworn off big-city
women. But his vow was about to be sorely tested when
he met Angel Wiley. Don't miss A RANCHING MAN
(IM #992), Linda Turner's next installment in her
Those Marrying McBrides! miniseries—
on sale in March 2000

And coming in June 2000, *Those Marrying McBrides!*
continues with Merry's story in
THE BEST MAN (IM #1010).
Available at your favorite retail outlet.

To order, send the completed form, along with a check or money order for the total
above, payable to Silhouette Books, to: **In the U.S.:** 3010 Walden Avenue, P.O. Box 9077,
Buffalo, NY 14269-9077; **In Canada:** P.O. Box 636, Fort Erie, Ontario, L2A 5X3.

Name: _____

Address: _____ City: _____

State/Prov.: _____ Zip/Postal Code: _____

Account # (if applicable): _____ 075 CSAS

*New York residents remit applicable sales taxes.
Canadian residents remit applicable
GST and provincial taxes.

Visit us at www.romance.net

SIMMCB

Silhouette ®
Where love comes alive™

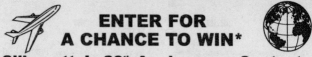

ENTER FOR A CHANCE TO WIN*

Silhouette's 20th Anniversary Contest

**Tell Us Where in the World
You Would Like *Your* Love To Come Alive...
And We'll Send the Lucky Winner There!**

Silhouette wants to take you wherever
your happy ending can come true.

Here's how to enter: Tell us, in 100 words or less,
where you want to go to make your love come alive!

In addition to the grand prize, there will be 200
runner-up prizes, collector's-edition book sets
autographed by one of the Silhouette anniversary
authors: **Nora Roberts, Diana Palmer,
Linda Howard** or **Annette Broadrick**.

DON'T MISS YOUR CHANCE TO WIN! ENTER NOW! No Purchase Necessary

Silhouette®
Where love comes alive™

Name:

Address:

City: State/Province:

Zip/Postal Code:

Mail to Harlequin Books: **In the U.S.:** P.O. Box 9069, Buffalo, NY
14269-9069; **In Canada:** P.O. Box 637, Fort Erie, Ontario, L4A 5X3

*No purchase necessary—for contest details send a self-addressed stamped envelope to:
Silhouette's 20th Anniversary Contest, P.O. Box 9069, Buffalo, NY, 14269-9069 (include
contest name on self-addressed envelope). Residents of Washington and Vermont may
omit postage. Open to Cdn. (excluding Quebec) and U.S. residents who are 18 or over.
Void where prohibited. Contest ends August 31, 2000.

PS20CON_R